I0541609

THE
MAYOR'S WIFE

ANNA KATHERINE GREEN

1st WORLD
LIBRARY
Literary Society

The Mayor's Wife

Anna Katherine Green

© 1st World Library, 2007
PO Box 2211
Fairfield, IA 52556
www.1stworldlibrary.com
First Edition

LCCN: 2007923731

Softcover ISBN: 978-1-4218-4223-3
Hardcover ISBN: 978-1-4218-4125-0
eBook ISBN: 978-1-4218-4321-6

Purchase *"The Mayor's Wife"*
as a traditional bound book at:
www.1stWorldLibrary.com/purchase.asp?ISBN=978-1-4218-4223-3

1st World Library is a literary, educational organization
dedicated to:

- Creating a free internet library of downloadable ebooks

  - Hosting writing competitions and offering book
    publishing scholarships.

Interested in more 1st World Library books?
contact: literacy@1stworldlibrary.com
Check us out at: www.1stworldlibrary.com

1ˢᵗ World Library Literary Society

Giving Back to the World

"If you want to work on the core problem, it's early school literacy."

- James Barksdale, former CEO of Netscape

"No skill is more crucial to the future of a child, or to a democratic and prosperous society, than literacy."

- Los Angeles Times

Literacy... means far more than learning how to read and write... The aim is to transmit... knowledge and promote social participation."

- UNESCO

"Literacy is not a luxury, it is a right and a responsibility. If our world is to meet the challenges of the twenty-first century we must harness the energy and creativity of all our citizens."

- President Bill Clinton

"Parents should be encouraged to read to their children, and teachers should be equipped with all available techniques for teaching literacy, so the varying needs and capacities of individual kids can be taken into account."

- Hugh Mackay

CONTENTS

CHAPTER I

A SPY'S DUTY

I am not without self-control, yet when Miss Davies entered the room with that air of importance she invariably assumes when she has an unusually fine position to offer, I could not hide all traces of my anxiety.

I needed a position, needed it badly, while the others—

But her eyes are on our faces, she is scanning us all with that close and calculating gaze which lets nothing escape. She has passed me by—my heart goes down, down—when suddenly her look returns and she singles me out.

"Miss Saunders." Then, "I have a word to say to you."

There is a rustle about me; five disappointed girls sink back into their seats as I quickly rise and follow Miss Davies out.

In the hall she faced me with these words:

"You are discreet, and you evidently desire a position. You will find a gentleman in my sitting-room. If you come to terms with him, well and good. If not, I shall expect you to forget all about him and his errand the moment you leave his presence. You understand me?"

"I think so," I replied, meeting her steady look with one

equally composed. Part of my strength—and I think I have some strength—lies in the fact that I am quietest when most deeply roused. "I am not to talk whatever the outcome."

"Not even to me," she emphasized.

Stirred still further and therefore outwardly even more calm than before, I stopped her as she was moving on and ventured a single query.

"This position—involving secrecy—is it one you would advise me to take, even if I did not stand in need of it so badly?"

"Yes. The difficulties will not be great to a discreet person. It is a first-class opportunity for a young woman as experienced as yourself."

"Thank you," was my abrupt but grateful rejoinder; and, obeying her silent gesture, I opened the door of the sitting-room and passed in. A gentleman standing at one of the windows turned quickly at the sound of my step and came forward. Instantly whatever doubt I may have felt concerning the nature of the work about to be proposed to me yielded to the certainty that, however much it might involve of the strange and difficult, the man whose mission it was to seek my aid was one to inspire confidence and respect.

He was also a handsome man, or no, I will not go so far as that; he was only one in whom the lines of form and visage were fine enough not to interfere with the impression made by his strong nature and intense vitality. A man to sway women and also quite capable of moving men (this was evident at a glance); but a man under a cloud just at present,—a very heavy cloud which both irked and perplexed him.

Pausing in the middle of the room, he surveyed me closely for an instant before speaking. Did I impress him as favorably as he did me? I soon had reason to think so, for the nervous trembling of his hands ceased after the first moment or two of

Anna Katherine Green

silent scrutiny, and I was sure I caught the note of hope in his voice as he courteously remarked:

"You are seeking a place, young lady. Do you think you can fill the one I have to offer? It has its difficulties, but it is not an onerous one. It is that of companion to my wife."

I bowed; possibly I smiled. I do smile sometimes when a ray of real sunshine darts across my pathway.

"I should be very glad to try such a situation," I replied.

A look of relief, so vivid that it startled me, altered at once the whole character of his countenance; and perceiving how intense was the power and fascination underlying his quiet exterior, I asked myself who and what this man was; no ordinary personage, I was sure, but who? Had Miss Davies purposely withheld his name? I began to think so.

"I have had some experience," I was proceeding—

But he waved this consideration aside, with a change back to his former gloomy aspect, and a careful glance at the door which did not escape me.

"It is not experience which is so much needed as discretion."

Again that word.

"The case is not a common one, or, rather,"—he caught himself up quickly, "the circumstances are not. My wife is well, but—she is not happy. She is very unhappy, deeply, unaccountably so, and I do not know why."

Anxious to watch the effect of these words, he paused a moment, then added fervently:

"Would to God I did! It would make a new man of me."

The meaning, the deep meaning in his tone, if not in the adjuration itself, was undeniable; but my old habit of self-control stood me in good stead and I remained silent and watchful, weighing every look and word.

"A week ago she was the lightest hearted woman in town,—the happiest wife, the merriest mother. To-day she is a mere wreck of her former self, pallid, drawn, almost speechless, yet she is not ill. She will not acknowledge to an ache or a pain; will not even admit that any change has taken place in her. But you have only to see her. And I am as ignorant of the cause of it all—as you are!" he burst out.

Still I remained silent, waiting, watchful.

"I have talked with her physician. He says there is something serious the matter with her, but he can not help her, as it is not in any respect physical, and advises me to find out what is on her mind. As if that had not been my first care! I have also consulted her most intimate friends, all who know her well, but they can give me no clue to her distress. They see the difference in her, but can not tell the cause. And I am obliged to go away and leave her in this state. For two weeks, three weeks now, my movements will be very uncertain. I am at the beck and call of the State Committee. At any other time I would try change of scene, but she will neither consent to leave home without me nor to interrupt my plans in order that I may accompany her."

"Miss Davies has not told me your name," I made bold to interpolate.

He stared, shook himself together, and quietly, remarked:

"I am Henry Packard."

The city's mayor! and not only that, the running candidate for governor. I knew him well by name, even if I did not know, or rather had not recognized his face.

Anna Katherine Green

"I beg pardon," I somewhat tremulously began, but he waved the coming apology aside as easily, as he had my first attempt at ingratiation. In fact, he appeared to be impatient of every unnecessary word. This I could, in a dim sort of way, understand. He was at the crisis of his fate, and so was his party. For several years a struggle had gone on between the two nearly matched elements in this western city, which, so far, had resulted in securing him two terms of office—possibly because his character appealed to men of all grades and varying convictions. But the opposite party was strong in the state, and the question whether he could carry his ticket against such odds, and thus give hope to his party in the coming presidential election, was one yet to be tested. Forceful as a speaker, he was expected to reap hundreds of votes from the mixed elements that invariably thronged to hear him, and, ignorant as I necessarily was of the exigencies of such a campaign, I knew that not only his own ambition, but the hopes of his party, depended on the speeches he had been booked to make in all parts of the state. And now, three weeks before election, while every opposing force was coming to the surface, this trouble had come upon him. A mystery in his home and threatened death in his heart! For he loved his wife—that was apparent to me from the first; loved her to idolatry, as such men sometimes do love,—often to their own undoing.

All this, the thought of an instant. Meanwhile he had been studying me well.

"You understand my position," he commented. "Wednesday night I speak in C—, Thursday, in R—, while she—" With an effort he pulled himself together. "Miss—"

"Saunders," I put in.

"Miss Saunders, I can not leave her alone in the house. Some one must be there to guard and watch—"

"Has she no mother?" I suggested in the pause he made.

"She has no living relatives, and mine are uncongenial to her."

This to save another question. I understood him perfectly.

"I can not ask any of them to stay with her," he pursued decisively. "She would not consent to it. Nor can I ask any of her friends. That she does not wish, either. But I can hire a companion. To that she has already consented. That she will regard as a kindness, if the lady chosen should prove to be one of those rare beings who carry comfort in their looks without obtruding their services or displaying the extent of their interest. You know there are some situations in which the presence of a stranger may be more grateful than that of a friend. Apparently, my wife feels herself so placed now."

Here his eyes again read my face, an ordeal out of which I came triumphant; the satisfaction he evinced rightly indicated his mind.

"Will you accept the position?" he asked. "We have one little child. You will have no charge of her save as you may wish to make use of her in reaching the mother."

The hint conveyed in the last phrase gave me courage to say:

"You wish me to reach her?"

"With comfort," said he.

"And if in doing so I learn her trouble?"

"You will win my eternal gratitude by telling it to one who would give ten years of his life to assuage it."

My head rose. I began to feel that my next step must strike solid ground.

"In other words to be quite honest—you wish me to learn her trouble if I can."

"I believe you can be trusted to do so."

"And then to reveal it to you?"

"If your sense of duty permits,—which I think it will."

I might have uttered in reply, "A spy's duty?" but the high-mindedness of his look forbade. Whatever humiliation his wishes put upon me, there could be no question of the uprightness of his motives regarding his wife.

I ventured one more question.

"How far shall I feel myself at liberty to go in this attempt?"

"As far as your judgment approves and circumstances seem to warrant. I know that you will come upon nothing dishonorable to her, or detrimental to our relations as husband and wife, in this secret which is destroying our happiness. Her affection for me is undoubted, but something—God knows what—has laid waste her life. To find and annihilate that something is my first and foremost duty. It does not fit well with those other duties pressing upon me from the political field, does it? That is why I have called in help. That is why I have called you in."

The emphasis was delicately but sincerely given. It struck my heart and entered it. Perhaps he had calculated upon this. If so, it was because he knew that a woman like myself works better when her feelings are roused.

Answering with a smile, I waited patiently while he talked terms and other equally necessary details, then dropping all these considerations, somewhat in his own grand manner, I made this remark:

"If your wife likes me, which very possibly she may fail to do, I shall have a few questions to ask you before I settle down to my duties. Will you see that an opportunity is given me for doing this?"

His assent was as frank as all the rest, and the next moment he left the room.

As he passed out I heard him remark to Miss Davies:

"I expect Miss Saunders at my house before nightfall. I shall reserve some minutes between half-past five and six in which to introduce her to Mrs. Packard."

CHAPTER II

QUESTIONS

I knew all the current gossip about Mrs. Packard before I had parted with Miss Davies. Her story was a simple one. Bred in the West, she had come, immediately after her mother's death, to live with that mother's brother in Detroit. In doing this she had walked into a fortune. Her uncle was a rich man and when he died, which was about a year after her marriage with Mr. Packard and removal to C—, she found herself the recipient of an enormous legacy. She was therefore a woman of independent means, an advantage which, added to personal attractions of a high order, and manners at once dignified and winning, caused her to be universally regarded as a woman greatly to be envied by all who appreciated a well-founded popularity.

So much for public opinion. It differs materially from that just given me by her husband.

The mayor lived on Franklin Street in a quarter I had seldom visited. As I entered this once aristocratic thoroughfare from Carlton Avenue, I was struck as I had been before by its heterogeneous appearance. Houses of strictly modern type neighbored those of a former period, and it was not uncommmon to see mansion and hovel confronting each other from the opposite side of the street. Should I find the number I sought attached to one of the crude, unmeaning dwellings I was constantly passing, or to one of mellower aspect and possibly historic association?

I own that I felt a decided curiosity on this point, and congratulated myself greatly when I had left behind me a peculiarly obnoxious monstrosity in stone, whose imposing proportions might reasonably commend themselves to the necessities, if not to the taste of the city's mayor.

A little shop, one story in height and old enough for its simple wooden walls to cry aloud for paint, stood out from the middle of a row of cheap brick houses. Directly opposite it were two conspicuous dwellings, neither of them new and one of them ancient as the street itself. They stood fairly close together, with an alley running between. From the number I had now reached it was evident that the mayor lived in one of these. Happily it was in the fresher and more inviting one. As I noted this, I paused in admiration of its spacious front and imposing doorway. The latter was in the best style of Colonial architecture, and though raised but one step from the walk, was so distinguished by the fan-tailed light overhead and the flanking casements glazed with antique glass, that I felt myself carried back to the days when such domiciles were few and denoted wealth the most solid, and hospitality the most generous.

A light wall, painted to match the house, extended without break to the adjoining building, a structure equal to the other in age and dimensions, but differing in all other respects as much as neglect and misuse could make it. Gray and forbidding, it towered in its place, a perfect foil to the attractive dwelling whose single step I now amounted with cheerful composure.

What should I have thought if at that moment I had been told that appearances were deceitful, and that there were many persons then living who, if left to their choice, would prefer life in the dismal walls from which I had instinctively turned, to a single night spent in the promising house I was so eager to enter.

An old serving-man, with a countenance which struck me

Anna Katherine Green

pleasantly enough at the time, opened the door in response to my ring, only to make instant way for Mayor Packard, who advanced from some near-by room to greet me. By this thoughtful attention I was spared the embarrassment from which I might otherwise have suffered.

His few words of greeting set me entirely at my ease, and I was quite ready to follow him when a moment later he invited me to meet Mrs. Packard.

"I can not promise you just the reception you naturally look for," said he, as he led me around the stairs toward an opening at their rear, "but she's a kind woman and can not but be struck with your own kind spirit and quiet manner."

Happily, I was not called upon to answer, for at that moment the door swung open and he ushered me into a room flooded brilliantly with the last rays of the setting sun. The woman who sat in its glow made an instant and permanent impression upon me. No one could look intently upon her without feeling that here was a woman of individuality and power, overshad-owed at present by the deepest melancholy. As she rose and faced us I decided instantly that her husband had not exaggerated her state of mind. Emotion of no ordinary nature disturbed the lines of her countenance and robbed her naturally fine figure of a goodly portion of its dignity and grace; and though she immediately controlled herself and assumed the imposing aspect of a highly trained woman, ready, if not eager, to welcome an intruding guest, I could not easily forget the drawn look about mouth and eyes which, in the first instant of our meeting, had distorted features naturally harmo-nious and beautifully serene.

I am sure her husband had observed it also, for his voice trembled slightly as he addressed her.

"I have brought you a companion, Olympia, one whose business and pleasure it will be to remain with you while I am making speeches a hundred miles away. Do you not see reason for thanking me?" This last question he pointed with a glance in my direction, which drew her attention and caused her to give me a kindly look.

I met her eyes fairly. They were large and gray and meant for smiling; eyes that, with a happy heart behind them, would illumine her own beauty and create joy in those upon whom they fell. But to-day, nothing but question lived in their dark and uneasy depths, and it was for me to face that question and give no sign of what the moment was to me.

"I think—I am sure, that my thanks are due you," she courteously replied, with a quick turn toward her husband, expressive of confidence, and, as I thought, of love. "I dreaded being left alone."

He drew a deep breath of relief; we both did; then we talked a little, after which Mayor Packard found some excuse for taking me from the room.

"Now for the few words you requested," said he; and, preceding me down the hall, he led me into what he called his study.

I noted one thing, and only one thing, on entering this place. That was the presence of a young man who sat at a distant table reading and making notes. But as Mayor Packard took no notice of him, knowing and expecting him to be there, no doubt, I, with a pardonable confusion, withdrew my eyes from the handsomest face I had ever seen, and, noting that my employer had stopped before a type-writer's table, I took my place at his side, without knowing very well what this move meant or what he expected me to do there.

I was not long left in doubt. With a gesture toward the type-writer, he asked me if I was accustomed to its use; and when I acknowledged some sort of acquaintance with it, he drew an unanswered letter from a pile on the table and requested me to copy it as a sample.

Anna Katherine Green

I immediately sat down before the type-writer. I was in something of a maze, but felt that I must follow his lead. As I proceeded to insert the paper and lay out the copy to hand, he crossed over to the young man at the other end of the room and began a short conversation which ended in some trivial demand that sent the young man from the room. As the door closed behind him Mayor Packard returned to my side.

"Keep on with your work and never mind mistakes," said he. "What I want is to hear the questions you told me to expect from you if you stayed."

Seemingly Mayor Packard did not wish this young man to know my position in the house. Was it possible he did not wholly trust him? My hands trembled from the machine and I was about to turn and give my full thought to what I had to say. But pride checked the impulse. "No," I muttered in quick dissuasion, to myself. "He must see that I can do two things at once and do both well." And so I went on with the letter.

"When," I asked, "did you first see the change in Mrs. Packard?"

"On Tuesday afternoon at about this time."

"What had happened on that day? Had she been out?"

"Yes, I think she told me later that she had been out."

"Do you know where?"

"To some concert, I believe. I did not press her with questions, Miss Saunders; I am a poor inquisitor."

Click, click; the machine was working admirably.

"Have you reason to think," I now demanded, "that she brought her unhappiness in with her, when she returned from that concert?"

"No; for when I returned home myself, as I did earlier than usual that night, I heard her laughing with the child in the nursery. It was afterward, some few minutes afterward, that I came upon her sitting in such a daze of misery, that she did not recognize me when I spoke to her. I thought it was a passing mood at the time; she is a sensitive woman and she had been reading—I saw the book lying on the floor at her side; but when, having recovered from her dejection—a dejection, mind you, which she would neither acknowledge nor explain—she accompanied me out to dinner, she showed even more feeling on our return, shrinking unaccountably from leaving the carriage and showing, not only in this way but in others, a very evident distaste to reenter her own house. Now, whatever hold I still retain upon her is of so slight a nature that I am afraid every day she will leave me."

"Leave you!"

My fingers paused; my astonishment had got the better of me.

"Yes; it is as bad as that. I don't know what day you will send me a telegram of three words, 'She has gone.' Yet she loves me, really and truly loves me. That is the mystery of it. More than this, her very heart-strings are knit up with those of our child."

"Mayor Packard,"—I had resumed work,—"was any letter delivered to her that day?"

"That I can not say."

Fact one for me to establish.

"The wives of men like you—men much before the world, men in the thick of strife, social and political—often receive letters of a very threatening character."

"She would have shown me any such, if only to put me on my guard. She is physically a very brave woman and not at all nervous."

"Those letters sometimes assume the shape of calumny. Your character may have been attacked."

"She believes in my character and would have given me an opportunity to vindicate myself. I have every confidence in my wife's sense of justice."

I experienced a thrill of admiration for the appreciation he evinced in those words. Yet I pursued the subject resolutely.

"Have you an enemy, Mayor Packard? Any real and downright enemy capable of a deep and serious attempt at destroying your happiness?"

"None that I know of, Miss Saunders. I have political enemies, of course men, who, influenced by party feeling, are not above attacking methods and possibly my official reputation; but personal ones—wretches willing to stab me in my home-life and affections, that I can not believe. My life has been as an open book. I have harmed no man knowingly and, as far as I know, no man has ever cherished a wish to injure me."

"Who constitute your household? How many servants do you keep and how long have they been with you?"

"Now you exact details with which only Mrs. Packard is conversant. I don't know anything about the servants. I do not interest myself much in matters purely domestic, and Mrs. Packard spares me. You will have to observe the servants yourself."

I made another note in my mind while inquiring:

"Who is the young man who was here just now? He has an uncommon face."

"A handsome one, do you mean?"

"Yes, and—well, what I should call distinctly clever."

"He is clever. My secretary, Miss Saunders. He helps me in my increased duties; has, in a way, charge of my campaign; reads, sorts and sometimes answers my letters. Just now he is arranging my speeches—fitting them to the local requirements of the several audiences I shall be called upon to address. He knows mankind like a book. I shall never give the wrong speech to the wrong people while he is with me."

"Do you like him?—the man, I mean, not his work."

"Well—yes. He is very good company, or would have been if, in the week he has been in the house, I had been in better mood to enjoy him. He's a capital story-teller."

"He has been here a week?"

"Yes, or almost."

"Came on last Tuesday, didn't he?"

"Yes, I believe that was the day."

"Toward afternoon?"

"No; he came early; soon after breakfast, in fact."

"Does your wife like him?"

His Honor gave a start, flushed (I can sometimes see a great deal even while very busily occupied) and answered without anger, but with a good deal of pride:

"I doubt if Mrs. Packard more than knows of his presence. She does not come to this room."

"And he does not sit at your table?"

"No; I must have some few minutes in the day free from the suggestion of politics. Mr. Steele can safely be left out of our discussion. He does not even sleep in the house."

The note I made at this was very emphatic. "You should know," said I; then quickly "Tuesday was the day Mrs. Packard first showed the change you observed in her."

"Yes, I think so; but that is a coincidence only. She takes no interest in this young man; scarcely noticed him when I introduced him; just bowed to him over her shoulder; she was fastening on our little one's cap. Usually she is extremely, courteous to strangers, but she was abstracted, positively abstracted at that moment. I wondered at it, for he usually makes a stir wherever he goes. But my wife cares little for beauty in a man; I doubt if she noticed his looks at all. She did not catch his name, I remember."

"Pardon me, what is that you say?"

"She did not catch his name, for later she asked me what it was."

"Tell me about that, Mr. Packard."

"It is immaterial; but I am ready to answer all your questions. It was while we were out dining. Chance threw us together, and to fill up the moment she asked the name of the young man I had brought into the library that morning. I told her and explained his position and the long training he had had in local politics. She listened, but not as closely as she did to the music. Oh, she takes no interest in him. I wish she did; his stories might amuse her."

I did not pursue the subject. Taking out the letter I had been writing, I held it out for his inspection, with the remark:

"More copy, please, Mayor Packard."

CHAPTER III

IN THE GABLE WINDOW

A few minutes later I was tripping up-stairs in the wake of a smart young maid whom Mayor Packard had addressed as Ellen. I liked this girl at first sight and, as I followed her up first one flight, then another, to the room which had been chosen for me, the hurried glimpses I had of her bright and candid face suggested that in this especial member of the household I might hope to find a friend and helper in case friendship and help were needed in the blind task to which I stood committed. But I soon saw cause—or thought I did—to change this opinion. When she turned on me at the door of my room, a small one at the extreme end of the third floor, I had an opportunity of meeting her eyes. The interest in her look was not the simple one to be expected. In another person in other circumstances I should have characterized her glance as one of inquiry and wonder. But neither inquiry nor wonder described the present situation, and I put myself upon my guard.

Seeing me look her way, she flushed, and, throwing wide the door, remarked in the pleasantest of tones:

"This is your room. Mrs. Packard says that if it is not large enough or does not seem pleasant to you, she will find you another one to-morrow."

"It's very pleasant and quite large enough," I confidently

Anna Katherine Green

replied, after a hasty look about me. "I could not be more comfortable."

She smiled, a trifle broadly for the occasion, I thought, and patted a pillow here and twitched a curtain there, as she remarked with a certain emphasis:

"I'm sure you will be comfortable. There's nobody else on this floor but Letty and the baby, but you don't look as if you would be easily frightened." Astonished, not so much by her words as by the furtive look she gave me, I laughed as I repeated "Frightened? What should frighten me?"

"Oh, nothing." Her back was to me now, but I felt that I knew her very look. "Nothing, of course. If you're not timid you won't mind sleeping so far away from every one. Then, we are always within call. The attic door is just a few steps off. We'll leave it unlocked and you can come up if—if you feel like it at any time. We'll understand."

Understand! I eyed her as she again looked my way, with some of her own curiosity if not wonder.

"Mrs. Packard must have had some very timorous guests," I observed. "Or, perhaps, you have had experiences here which have tended to alarm you. The house is so large and imposing for the quarter it is in I can readily imagine it to attract burglars."

"Burglars! It would be a brave burglar who would try to get in here. I guess you never heard about this house."

"No," I admitted, unpleasantly divided between a wish to draw her out and the fear of betraying Mayor Packard's trust in me by showing the extent of my interest.

"Well, it's only gossip," she laughingly assured me. "You needn't think of it, Miss. I'm sure you'll be all right. We girls have been, so far, and Mrs. Packard—"

Here she doubtless heard a voice outside or some summons from below, for she made a quick start toward the door, remarking in a different and very pleasant tone of voice:

"Dinner at seven, Miss. There'll be no extra company to-night. I'm coming." This to some one in the hall as she hastily passed through the door.

Dropping the bag I had lifted to unpack, I stared at the door which had softly closed under her hand, then, with an odd impulse, turned to look at my own face in the glass before which I chanced to be standing. Did I expect to find there some evidence of the excitement which this strange conversation might naturally produce in one already keyed up to an expectation of the mysterious and unusual? If so, I was not disappointed. My features certainly betrayed the effect of this unexpected attack upon my professional equanimity. What did the girl mean? What was she hinting at? What underlay—what could underlie her surprising remark, "I guess you never heard about this house"? Something worth my knowing; something which might explain Mayor Packard's fears and Mrs. Packard's—

There I stopped. It was where the girl had stopped. She and not I must round out this uncompleted sentence.

Meanwhile I occupied myself in unpacking my two bags and making acquaintance with the room which, I felt, was destined to be the scene of many, anxious thoughts. Its first effect had been a cheerful one, owing to its two large windows, one looking out on a stretch of clear sky above a mass of low, huddled buildings, and the other on the wall of the adjacent house which, though near enough to obstruct the view, was not near enough to exclude all light. Another and closer scrutiny of the room did not alter the first impression. To the advantages of light were added those of dainty furnishing and an exceptionally pleasing color scheme. There was no richness anywhere, but an attractive harmony which gave one an instantaneous feeling of home. From the little brass bedstead

Anna Katherine Green

curtained with cretonne, to the tiny desk filled with everything needful for immediate use, I saw evidences of the most careful housekeeping, and was vainly asking myself what could have come into Mrs. Packard's life to disturb so wholesome a nature, when my attention was arrested by a picture hanging at the right of the window overlooking the next house.

It gave promise of being a most interesting sketch, and I crossed over to examine it; but instead of doing so, found my eyes drawn toward something more vital than any picture and twice as enchaining.

It was a face, the face of an old woman staring down at me from a semicircular opening in the gable of the adjoining house. An ordinary circumstance in itself, but made extraordinary by the fixity of her gaze, which was leveled straight on mine, and the uncommon expression of breathless eagerness which gave force to her otherwise commonplace features. So remarkable was this expression and so apparently was it directed against myself, that I felt like throwing up my window and asking the poor old creature what I could do for her. But her extreme immobility deterred me. For all the intentness of her look there was no invitation in it warranting such an advance on my part. She simply stared down at me in unbroken anxiety, nor, though I watched her for some minutes with an intensity equal to her own, did I detect any change either in her attitude or expression.

"Odd," thought I, and tested her with a friendly bow. The demonstration failed to produce the least impression. "A most uncanny neighbor," was my mental comment on finally turning away. Truly I was surrounded by mysteries, but fortunately this was one with which I had no immediate concern. It did not take me long to put away my few belongings and prepare for dinner. When quite ready, I sat down to write a letter. This completed, I turned to go downstairs. But before leaving the room I cast another look up at my neighbor's attic window. The old woman was still there. As our glances met I experienced a thrill which was hardly one of sympathy, yet was not exactly one of fear. My impulse was to pull down the shade between us, but I had not the heart. She was so old, so feeble and so, evidently the prey of some strange and fixed idea. What idea? It was not for me to say, but I found it impossible to make any move which would seem to shut her out; so I left the shade up; but her image followed me and I forgot it only when confronted once again with Mrs. Packard.

That lady was awaiting me at the dining-room door. She had succeeded in throwing off her secret depression and smiled quite naturally as I approached. Her easy, courteous manners became her wonderfully. I immediately recognized how much there was to admire in our mayor's wife, and quite understood his relief when, a few minutes later, we sat at table and conversation began. Mrs. Packard, when free and light-hearted, was a delightful companion and the meal passed off cheerily. When we rose and the mayor left us for some necessary business it was with a look of satisfaction in my direction which was the best possible preparation for my approaching tete-a-tete with his moody and incomprehensible wife.

But I was not destined to undergo the contemplated ordeal this evening. Guests were announced whom Mrs. Packard kindly invited me to meet, but I begged to be allowed to enjoy the library. I had too much to consider just now, to find any pleasure in society. Three questions filled my mind.

What was Mrs. Packard's secret trouble?

Why were people afraid to remain in this house?

Why did the old woman next door show such interest in the new member of her neighbor's household?

Would a single answer cover all? Was there but one cause for each and every one of these peculiarities? Probably, and it was my duty to ferret out this cause. But how should I begin? I remembered what I had read about detectives and their methods, but the help I thus received was small. Subtler methods were demanded here and subtler methods I must find. Meantime, I would hope for another talk with Mayor Packard. He might clear up some of this fog. At least, I should like to give him the opportunity. But I saw no way of reaching him at present. Even Mrs. Packard did not feel at liberty to disturb him in his study. I must wait for his reappearance, and in the meantime divert myself as best I could. I caught up a magazine, but speedily dropped it to cast a quick glance around the room. Had I heard anything? No. The house was perfectly still, save for the sound of conversation in the drawing-room. Yet I found it hard to keep my eyes upon the page. Quite without my volition they flew, first to one corner, then to another. The room was light, there were no shadowy nooks in it, yet I felt an irresistible desire to peer into every place not directly under my eye. I knew it to be folly, and, after succumbing to the temptation of taking a sly look behind a certain tall screen, I resolutely set myself to curb my restless-ness and to peruse in good earnest the article I had begun. To make sure of myself, I articulated each word aloud, and to my exceeding satisfaction had reached the second column when I found my voice trailing off into silence, and every sense alarmingly alert. Yet there was nothing, absolutely nothing in this well-lighted, cozy family-room to awaken fear. I was sure of this the next minute, and felt correspondingly irritated with myself and deeply humiliated. That my nerves should play me such a trick at the very outset of my business in this house! That I could not be left alone, with life in every part of the house, and the sound of the piano and cheerful talking just across the hall, without the sense of the morbid and unearthly entering my matter-of-fact brain!

Uttering an ejaculation of contempt, I reseated myself. The impulse came again to look behind me, but I mastered it this time without too great an effort. I already knew every feature of the room: its old-fashioned mantel, large round center-table, its couches and chairs, and why should I waste my attention again upon them?

"Is there anything you wish, Miss?" asked a voice directly over my shoulder.

I wheeled about with a start. I had heard no one approach; it was not sound which had disturbed me.

"The library bell rang," continued the voice. "Is it ice-water you want?"

Then I saw that it was Nixon, the butler, and shook my head in mingled anger and perplexity; for not only had he advanced quite noiselessly, but he was looking at me with that curious concentrated gaze which I had met twice before since coming into this house.

"I need nothing," said I, with all the mildness I could summon into my voice; and did not know whether to like or not like the quiet manner in which he sidled out of the room.

"Why do they all look at me so closely?" I queried, in genuine confusion. "The man had no business here. I did not ring, and I don't believe he thought I did. He merely wanted to see what I was doing and whether I was enjoying myself. Why this curiosity? I have never roused it anywhere else. It is not myself they are interested in, but the cause and purpose of my presence under this roof." I paused to wonder over the fact that the one member of the family who might be supposed to resent my intrusion most was the one who took it most kindly and with least token of surprise—Mrs. Packard.

"She accepts me easily enough," thought I. "To her I am a welcome companion. What am I to these?"

The answer, or rather a possible answer, came speedily. At nine o'clock Mayor Packard entered the room from his study across the hall, and, seeing me alone, came forward briskly. "Mrs. Packard has company and I am on my way to the drawing-room, but I am happy to have the opportunity of assuring you that already she looks better, and that I begin to hope that your encouraging presence may stimulate her to throw aside her gloom and needless apprehensions. I shall be eternally grateful to you if it will. It is the first time in a week that she has consented to receive visitors." I failed to feel the same elation over this possibly temporary improvement in his wife's condition, but I carefully refrained from betraying my doubts. On the contrary, I took advantage of the moment to clear my mind of one of the many perplexities disturbing it.

"And I am glad of this opportunity to ask you what may seem a foolish, if not impertinent question. The maid, Ellen, in showing me my room, was very careful to assure me that she slept near me and would let me into her room in case I experienced any alarm in the night; and when I showed surprise at her expecting me to feel alarm of any kind in a house full of people, made the remark, 'I guess you do not know about this house.' Will you pardon me if I ask if there is anything I don't know, and should know, about the home your suffering wife inhabits? A problem such as you have given me to solve demands a thorough understanding of every cause capable of creating disturbance in a sensitive mind."

The mayor's short laugh failed to hide his annoyance. "You will find nothing in this direction," said he, "to account for the condition I have mentioned to you. Mrs. Packard is utterly devoid of superstition. That I made sure of before signing the lease of this old house. But I forgot; you are doubtless ignorant of its reputation. It has, or rather has had, the name of being haunted. Ridiculous, of course, but a fact with which Mrs. Packard has had to contend in"—he gave me a quick glance— "in hiring servants."

It was now my turn to smile, but somehow I did not. A vision had risen in my mind of that blank and staring face in the attic window next door, and I felt—well, I don't know how I felt, but I did not smile.

Another short laugh escaped him.

"We have not been favored by any manifestations from the spiritual world. This has proved a very matter-of-fact sort of home for us. I had almost forgotten that it was burdened with such an uncanny reputation, and I'm sure that Mrs. Packard would have shared my indifference if it had not been for the domestic difficulty I have mentioned. It took us two weeks to secure help of any kind."

"Indeed! and how long have you been in the house? I judge that you rent it?"

"Yes, we rent it and we have been here two months. It was the only house I could get in a locality convenient for me; besides, the old place suits me. It would take more than an obsolete ghost or so to scare me away from what I like."

"But Mrs. Packard? She may not be a superstitious woman, yet—"

"Don't be fanciful, Miss Saunders. You will have to look deeper than that for the spell which has been cast over my wife. Olympia afraid of creaks and groans? Olympia seeing sights? She's much too practical by nature, Miss Saunders, to say nothing of the fact that she would certainly have confided her trouble to me, had her imagination been stirred in this way. Little things have invariably been discussed between us. I repeat that this possibility should not give you a moment's thought."

A burst of sweet singing came from the drawing-room.

"That's her voice," he cried. "Whatever her trouble may be she has forgotten it for the moment. Excuse me if I join her. It is such pleasure to have her at all like herself again."

I longed to detain him, longed to put some of the numberless questions my awakened curiosity demanded, but his impatience was too marked and I let him depart without another word.

But I was not satisfied. Inwardly I determined to see him again as soon as possible and gain a more definite insight into the mysteries of his home.

CHAPTER IV

LIGHTS—SOUNDS

I am by nature a thoroughly practical woman. If I had not been, the many misfortunes of my life would have made me so. Yet, when the library door closed behind the mayor and I found myself again alone in a spot where I had not felt comfortable from the first, I experienced an odd sensation not unlike fear. It left me almost immediately and my full reasoning powers reasserted themselves; but the experience had been mine and I could not smile it away.

The result was a conviction, which even reason could not dispel, that whatever secret tragedy or wrong had signalized this house, its perpetration had taken place in this very room. It was a fancy, but it held, and under its compelling if irrational influence, I made a second and still more minute survey of the room to which this conviction had imparted so definite an interest.

I found it just as ordinary and unsuggestive as before; an old-fashioned, square apartment renovated and redecorated to suit modern tastes. Its furnishings I have already described; they were such as may be seen in any comfortable abode. I did not linger over them a moment; besides, they were the property of the present tenant, and wholly disconnected with the past I was insensibly considering. Only the four walls and what they held, doors, windows and mantel-piece, remained to speak of those old days. Of the doors there were two, one opening into

Anna Katherine Green

the main hall under the stairs, the other into a cross corridor separating the library from the dining-room. It was through the dining-room door Nixon had come when he so startled me by speaking unexpectedly over my shoulder! The two windows faced the main door, as did the ancient, heavily carved mantel. I could easily imagine the old-fashioned shutters hidden behind the modern curtains, and, being anxious to test the truth of my imaginings, rose and pulled aside one of these curtains only to see, just as I expected, the blank surface of a series of unslatted shutters, tightly fitting one to another with old-time exactitude. A flat hook and staple fastened them. Gently raising the window, and lifting one, I pulled the shutter open and looked out. The prospect was just what I had been led to expect from the location of the room—the long, bare wall of the neighboring house. I was curious about that house, more curious at this moment than ever before; for though it stood a good ten feet away from the one I was now in, great pains had been taken by its occupants to close every opening which might invite the glances of a prying eye. A door which had once opened on the alley running between the two houses had been removed and its place boarded up. So with a window higher up; the half-circle window near the roof, I could not see from my present point of view.

Drawing back, I reclosed the shutter, lowered the window and started for my own room. As I passed the first stair-head, I heard a baby's laugh, followed by a merry shout, which, ringing through the house, seemed to dispel all its shadows.

I had touched reality again. Remembering Mayor Packard's suggestion that I might through the child find a means of reaching the mother, I paid a short visit to the nursery where I found a baby whose sweetness must certainly have won its mother's deepest love. Letty, the nurse, was of a useful but commonplace type, a conscientious nurse, that was all.

But I was to have a further taste of the unusual that night and to experience another thrill before I slept. My room was dark when I entered it, and, recognizing a condition favorable to the gratification of my growing curiosity in regard to the neighboring house, I approached the window and stole a quick look at the gable-end where, earlier in the evening I had seen peering out at me an old woman's face. Conceive my astonishment at finding the spot still lighted and a face looking out, but not the same face, a countenance as old, one as intent, but of different conformation and of a much more intellectual type. I considered myself the victim of an illusion; I tried to persuade myself that it was the same woman, only in another garb and under a different state of feeling; but the features were much too dissimilar for such an hypothesis to hold. The eagerness, the unswerving attitude were the same, but the first woman had had a weak round face with pinched features, while this one showed a virile head and long heavy cheeks and chin, which once must have been full of character, though they now showed only heaviness of heart and the dull apathy of a fixed idea.

Two women, total strangers to me, united in an unceasing watch upon me in my room! I own that the sense of mystery which this discovery brought struck me at the moment as being fully as uncanny and as unsettling to contemplate as the idea of a spirit haunting walls in which I was destined for a while to live, breathe and sleep. However, as soon as I had drawn the shade and lighted the gas, I forgot the whole thing, and not till I was quite ready for bed, and my light again turned low, did I feel the least desire to take another peep at that mysterious window. The face was still there, peering at me through a flood of moonlight. The effect was ghastly, and for hours I could not sleep, imagining that face still staring down upon me, illuminated with the unnatural light and worn with a profitless and unmeaning vigil.

That there was something to fear in this house was evident from the halting step with which the servants, one and all, passed my door on their way up to their own beds. I now knew, or thought I knew, what was in their minds; but the comfort brought by this understanding was scarcely sufficient to act as antidote to the keen strain to which my faculties had been brought. Yet nothing happened, and when a clock somewhere in the house had assured me by its own clear stroke that the dreaded midnight hour had passed I rose and stole again to the window. This time both moonlight and face were gone. Contentment came with the discovery. I crept back to bed with lightened heart and soon was asleep.

Next morning, however, the first face was again at the window, as I at once saw on raising the blind. I breakfasted alone. Mrs. Packard was not yet down and the mayor had already left to fulfil an early appointment down-town. Old Nixon waited on me. As he, like every other member of the family, with the possible exception of the mayor, was still an unknown quantity in the problem given me to solve, I allowed a few stray glances to follow him as he moved decorously about the board anticipating my wants and showing himself an adept in his appointed task. Once I caught his eye and I half expected him to speak, but he was too well-trained for that, and the meal proceeded in the same silence in which it had begun. But this short interchange of looks had given me an idea. He showed an eager interest in me quite apart from his duty to me as waiter. He was nearer sixty, than fifty, but it was not his age which made his hand tremble as he laid down a plate before me or served me with coffee and bread. Whether this interest was malevolent or kindly I found it impossible to judge. He had a stoic's face with but one eloquent feature—his eyes; and these he kept studiously lowered after that one quick glance. Would it help matters for me to address him? Possibly, but I decided not to risk it. Whatever my immediate loss I must on no account rouse the least distrust in this evidently watchful household. If knowledge came naturally, well and good; I must not seem to seek it.

The result proved my discretion. As I was rising from the table Nixon himself made this remark:

"Mrs. Packard will be glad to see you in her room up-stairs any time after ten o'clock. Ellen will show you where." Then, as I was framing a reply, he added in a less formal tone: "I hope you were not disturbed last night. I told the girls not to be so noisy."

Now they had been very quiet, so I perceived that he simply wanted to open conversation.

"I slept beautifully," I assured him. "Indeed, I'm not easily kept awake. I don't believe I could keep awake if I knew that a ghost would stalk through my room at midnight."

His eyes opened, and he did just what I had intended him to do,—met my glance directly.

"Ghosts!" he repeated, edging uneasily forward, perhaps with the intention of making audible his whisper: "Do you believe in ghosts?"

I laughed easily and with a ringing merriment, like the light-hearted girl I should be and am not.

"No," said I, "why should I? But I should like to. I really should enjoy the experience of coming face to face with a wholly shadowless being."

He stared and now his eyes told nothing. Mechanically I moved to go, mechanically he stepped aside to give me place. But his curiosity or his interest would not allow him to see me pass out without making another attempt to understand me. Stammering in his effort to seem indifferent, he dropped this quiet observation just as I reached the door.

"Some people say, or at least I have heard it whispered in the neighborhood, that this house is haunted. I've never seen anything, myself."

I forced myself to give a tragic start (I was half ashamed of my arts), and, coming back, turned a purposely excited countenance toward him.

"This house!" I cried. "Oh, how lovely! I never thought I should have the good fortune of passing the night in a house that is really haunted. What are folks supposed to see? I don't know much about ghosts out of books."

This nonplussed him. He was entirely out of his element. He glanced nervously at the door and tried to seem at his ease; perhaps tried to copy my own manner as he mumbled these words:

"I've not given much attention to the matter, Miss. It's not long since we came here and Mrs. Packard don't approve of our gossiping with the neighbors. But I think the people have mostly been driven away by strange noises and by lights which no one could explain, flickering up over the ceilings from the halls below. I don't want to scare you, Miss—"

"Oh, you won't scare me."

"Mrs. Packard wouldn't like me to do that. She never listens to a word from us about these things, and we don't believe the half of it ourselves; but the house does have a bad name, and it's the wonder of everybody that the mayor will live in it."

"Sounds?" I repeated. "Lights?"—and laughed again. "I don't think I shall bother myself about them!" I went gaily out.

It did seem very puerile to me, save as it might possibly account in some remote way for Mrs. Packard's peculiar mental condition.

Up-stairs I found Ellen. She was in a talkative mood, and this time I humored her till she had told me all she knew about the house and its ghostly traditions. This all had come from a servant, a nurse who had lived in the house before. Ellen herself, like the butler, Nixon, had had no personal experiences to relate, though the amount of extra wages she received had quite prepared her for them. Her story, or rather the nurse's story, was to the following effect.

The house had been built and afterward inhabited for a term of years by one of the city fathers, a well-known and still widely remembered merchant. No unusual manifestations had marked it during his occupancy. Not till it had run to seed and been the home of decaying gentility, and later of actual poverty, did it acquire a name which made it difficult to rent, though the neighborhood was a growing one and the house itself well-enough built to make it a desirable residence. Those who had been induced to try living within its spacious walls invariably left at the end of the month. Why, they hesitated to say; yet if pressed would acknowledge that the rooms were full of terrible sights and sounds which they could not account for; that a presence other than their own was felt in the house; and that once (every tenant seemed to be able to cite one instance) a hand had touched them or a breath had brushed their cheek which had no visible human source, and could be traced to no mortal presence. Not much in all this, but it served after a while to keep the house empty, while its reputation for mystery did not lie idle. Sounds were heard to issue from it. At times lights were seen glimmering through this or that chink or rift in the window curtain, but by the time the door was unlocked and people were able to rush in, the interior was still and dark and seemingly untouched. Finally the police took a hand in the matter. They were on the scent just then of a party of counterfeiters and were suspicious of the sounds and lights in this apparently unoccupied dwelling. But they watched and waited in vain. One of them got a scare and that was all. The mystery went unsolved and the sign "To Let" remained indefinitely on the house-front.

At last a family from the West decided to risk the terrors of this domicile. The nurse, whose story I was listening to, came with them and entered upon her duties without prejudice or any sort of belief in ghosts, general or particular. She held this belief just two weeks. Then her incredulity began to waver. In fact, she saw the light; almost saw the ghost, certainly saw the ghost's penumbra. It was one night, or rather very early, one morning. She had been sitting up with the baby, who had been suffering from a severe attack of croup. Hot water was wanted, and she started for the kitchen for the purpose of making a fire and putting on the kettle. The gas had not been lit in the hall—they had all been too busy, and she was feeling her way down the front stairs with a box of matches in her hand, when suddenly she heard from somewhere below a sound which she could never describe, and at the same moment saw a light which spread itself through all the lower hall so that every object stood out distinctly.

She did not think of the ghost at first, her thoughts were so full of the child; but when a board creaked in the hall floor, a board that always creaked when stepped on, she remembered the reputation and what had been told her about a creaking board and a light that came and went without human agency. Frightened for a minute, she stood stock-still, then she rushed down. Whatever it was, natural or supernatural, she went to see it; but the light vanished before she passed the lower stair, and only a long-drawn sigh not far from her ear warned her that the space between her and the real hall was not the solitude she was anxious to consider it. A sigh! That meant a person. Striking a match, she looked eagerly down the hall. Something was moving between the two walls. But when she tried to determine its character, it was swallowed up in darkness,—the match had gone out. Anxious for the child and determined to go her way to the kitchen, she now felt about for the gas-fixture and succeeded in lighting up. The whole hall again burst into view but the thing was no longer there; the space was absolutely empty. And so were the other rooms, for she went into every one, lighting the gas as she went; and so was the cellar when she reached it. For she had to go to its extreme length for wood and wait about the kitchen till the water boiled, during which time she searched every nook and cranny. Oh, she was a brave woman, but she did have this thought as she went upstairs: If the child died she would know that she had seen a spirit; if the child got well, that she had been the victim of her own excitement.

And did the child die?

"No, it got well, but the family moved out as soon as it was safe to leave the house. Her employees did not feel as easy about the matter as she did."

CHAPTER V

THE STRANGE NEIGHBORS NEXT DOOR

When I joined Mrs. Packard I found her cheerful and in all respects quite unlike the brooding woman she had seemed when I first met her. From the toys scattered about her feet I judged that the child had been with her, and certainly the light in her eyes had the beaming quality we associate with the happy mother. She was beautiful thus and my hopes of her restoration to happiness rose.

"I have had a good night," were her first words as she welcomed me to a seat in her own little nook. "I'm feeling very well this morning. That is why I have brought out this big piece of work." She held up a baby's coat she was embroidering. "I can not do it when I am nervous. Are you ever nervous?"

Delighted to enter into conversation with her, I answered in a way to lead her to talk about herself, then, seeing she was in a favorable mood for gossip, was on the point of venturing all in a leading question, when she suddenly forestalled me by putting one to me.

"Were you ever the prey of an idea?" she asked; "one which you could not shake off by any ordinary means, one which clung to you night and day till nothing else seemed real or would rouse the slightest interest? I mean a religious idea," she stammered with anxious attempt of to hide her real thought.

"One of those doubts which come to you in the full swing of life to—to frighten and unsettle you."

"Yes," I answered, as naturally and quietly as I knew how; "I have had such ideas—such doubts."

"And were you able to throw them off?—by your will, I mean."

She was leaning forward, her eyes fixed eagerly on mine. How unexpected the privilege! I felt that in another moment her secret would be mine.

"In time, yes," I smiled back. "Everything yields to time and persistent conscientious work."

"But if you can not wait for time, if you must be relieved at once, can the will be made to suffice, when the day is dark and one is alone and not too busy?"

"The will can do much," I insisted. "Dark thoughts can be kept down by sheer determination. But it is better to fill the mind so full with what is pleasant that no room is left for gloom. There is so much to enjoy it must take a real sorrow to disturb a heart resolved to be happy."

"Yes, resolved to be happy. I am resolved to be happy." And she laughed merrily for a moment. "Nothing else pays. I will not dwell on anything but the pleasures which surround me." Here she took up her work again. "I will forget—I will—" She stopped and her eyes left her work to flash a rapid and involuntary glance over her shoulder. Had she heard a step? I had not. Or had she felt a draft of which I in my bounding health was unconscious?

"Are you cold?" I asked, as her glance stole back to mine. "You are shivering—"

"Oh, no," she answered coldly, almost proudly. "I'm perfectly

Anna Katherine Green

warm. I don't feel slight changes. I thought some one was behind me. I felt—Is Ellen in the adjoining room?"

I jumped up and moved toward the door she indicated. It was slightly ajar, but Ellen was not behind it.

"There's no one here," said I.

She did not answer. She was bending again over her work, and gave no indication of speaking again on that or the more serious topic we had previously been discussing.

Naturally I felt disappointed. I had hoped much from the conversation, and now these hopes bade fair to fail me. How could I restore matters to their former basis? Idly I glanced out of the side window I was passing, and the view of the adjoining house I thus gained acted like an inspiration. I would test her on a new topic, in the hope of reintroducing the old. The glimpse I had gained into Mrs. Packard's mind must not be lost quite as soon as this.

"You asked me a moment ago if I were ever nervous," I began, as I regained my seat at her side. "I replied, 'Sometimes'; but I might have said if I had not feared being too abrupt, 'Never till I came into this house.'"

Her surprise partook more of curiosity than I expected.

"You are nervous here," she repeated. "What is the reason of that, pray? Has Ellen been chattering to you? I thought she knew enough not to do that. There's nothing to fear here, Miss Saunders; absolutely nothing for you to fear. I should not have allowed you to remain here a night if there had been. No ghost will visit you."

"No, I hear they never wander above the second story," I laughed. "If they did I should hardly anticipate the honor of a visit. It is not ghosts I fear; it is something quite different which affects me,—living eyes, living passions, the old ladies next door," I finished falteringly, for Mrs. Packard was looking at me with a show of startling alarm. "They stare into my room night and day. I never look out but I encounter the uncanny glance of one or the other of them. Are they live women or embodied memories of the past? They don't seem to belong to the present. I own that they frighten me."

I had exaggerated my feelings in order to mark their effect upon her. The result disappointed me; she was not afraid of these two poor old women. Far from it.

"Draw your curtains," she laughed. "The poor things are crazy and not really accountable. Their odd ways and manners troubled me at first, but I soon got over it. I have even been in to see them. That was to keep them from coming here. I think if you were to call upon them they would leave you alone after that. They are very fond of being called on. They are persons of the highest gentility, you know. They owned this house a few years ago, as well as the one they are now living in, but misfortunes overtook them and this one was sold for debt. I am very sorry for them myself. Sometimes I think they have not enough to eat."

"Tell me about them," I urged. Lightly as she treated the topic I felt convinced that these strange neighbors of hers were more or less involved in the mystery of her own peculiar moods and unaccountable fears.

"It's a great secret," she announced naively. "That is, their personal history. I have never told it to any one. I have never told it to my husband. They confided it to me in a sort of desperation, perhaps because my husband's name inspired them with confidence. Immediately after, I could see that they regretted the impulse, and so I have remained silent. But I feel like telling you; feel as if it would divert me to do so—keep me from thinking of other things. You won't want to talk about it and the story will cure your nervousness."

"Do you want me to promise not to talk about it?" I inquired in some anxiety.

"No. You have a good, true face; a face which immediately inspires confidence. I shall exact no promises. I can rely on your judgment."

I thanked her. I was glad not to be obliged to promise secrecy. It might become my imperative duty to disregard such a promise.

"You have seen both of their faces?" she asked.

I nodded.

"Then you must have observed the difference between them. There is the same difference in their minds, though both are clouded. One is weak almost to the point of idiocy, though strong enough where her one settled idea is concerned. The other was once a notable character, but her fine traits have almost vanished under the spell which has been laid upon them by the immense disappointment which has wrecked both their lives. I heard it all from Miss Thankful the day after we entered this house. Miss Thankful is the older and more intellectual one. I had known very little about them before; no more, in fact, than I have already told you. I was consequently much astonished when they called, for I had supposed them to be veritable recluses, but I was still more astonished when I noted their manner and the agitated and strangely penetrating looks they cast about them as I ushered them into the library, which was the only room I had had time to arrange. A few minutes' further observation of them showed me that neither of them was quite right. Instead of entering into conversation with me they continued to cast restless glances at the walls, ceilings, and even at the floor of the room in which we sat, and when, in the hope of attracting their attention to myself, I addressed them on some topic which I thought would be interesting to them, they not only failed to listen, but turned upon each other with slowly wagging heads, which not only revealed their condition but awakened me to its probable cause. They were between walls rendered dear by old associations. Till their first agitation was over I could not hope for their attention.

"But their agitation gave no signs of diminishing and I soon saw that their visit was far from being a ceremonial one; that it was one of definite purpose. Preparing myself for I knew not what, I regarded them with such open interest that before I knew it, and quite before I was ready for any such exhibition, they were both on their knees before me, holding up their meager arms with beseeching and babbling words which I did not understand till later.

"I was shocked, as you may believe, and quickly raised them, at which Miss Thankful told me their story, which I will now tell you.

"There were four of them originally, three sisters and one brother. The brother early went West and disappeared out of their lives, and the third sister married. This was years and years ago, when they were all young. From this marriage sprang all their misfortune. The nephew which this marriage introduced to their family became their bane as well as their delight. From being a careless spendthrift boy he became a reckless, scheming man, adding extravagance to extravagance, till, to support him and meet his debts, these poor aunts gave up first their luxuries, then their home and finally their very livelihood. Not that they acknowledged this. The feeling they both cherished for him was more akin to infatuation than to ordinary family love. They did not miss their luxuries, they did not mourn their home, they did not even mourn their privations; but they were broken-hearted and had been so for a long time, because they could no longer do for him as of old. Shabby themselves, and evidently ill-nourished, they grieved not over their own changed lot, but over his. They could not be reconciled to his lack of luxuries, much less to the difficulties in which he frequently found himself, who was made to ruffle it with the best and be the pride of their lives as he was the darling of their hearts. All this the poor old things made apparent to me, but their story did not become really interesting till they began to speak of this house we are in, and of certain events which followed their removal to the ramshackle dwelling next door. The sale of this portion of the property had relieved them from their debts, but they were otherwise penniless, and were just planning the renting of their rooms at prices which would barely serve to provide them with a scanty living, when there came a letter from their graceless nephew, asking for a large amount of money to save him from complete disgrace. They had no money, and were in the midst of their sorrow and perplexity, when a carriage drove up to the door of this house and from it issued an old and very sick man, their long absent and almost forgotten brother. He had come home to die, and when told his sisters' circumstances, and how soon the house next door would be filled with lodgers, insisted upon having this place of his birth, which was empty at the time, opened for his use. The owner, after long continued entreaties from the poor old sisters, finally consented to the arrangement. A bed was made up in the library, and the old man laid on it."

Mrs. Packard's voice fell, and I cast her a humorous look.

"Were there ghosts in those days?" I lightly asked.

Her answer was calm enough. "Not yet, but the place must have been desolate enough for one. I have sometimes tried to imagine the scene surrounding that broken-down old man. There was no furniture in the room, save what was indispensable to his bare comfort. Miss Thankful expressly said there was no carpet,—you will presently see why. Even the windows had no other protection than the bare shutters. But he was in his old home, and seemed content till Miss Charity fell sick, and they had to call in a nurse to assist Miss Thankful, who by this time had a dozen lodgers to look after. Then he grew very restless. Miss Thankful said he seemed to be afraid of this nurse, and always had a fever after having been left alone with her; but he gave no reason for his fears, and she herself was too straitened in means and in too much trouble otherwise to be affected by such mere whims, and went on doing her best, sitting with him whenever the opportunity offered, and making every effort to conceal the anxiety she felt for her poor nephew from her equally poor brother. The disease under which the brother labored was a fatal one, and he had not many days to live. She was startled when one day her brother greeted her appearance, with an earnest entreaty for the nurse to be sent out for a little while, as this was his last day, and he had something of great importance to communicate to her before he died.

"She had not dreamed of his being so low as this, but when she came to look at him, she saw, that he had not misstated his case, and that he was really very near death. She was in a flurry and wanted to call in the neighbors and rout her sister up from her own sick bed to care for him. But he wanted nothing and nobody, only to be left alone with her.

"So she sent the nurse out and sat down on the side of the bed to hear what he had to say to her, for he looked very eager and was smiling in a way to make her heart ache.

"You must remember," continued Mrs. Packard, "that at the time Miss Thankful was telling this story we were in the very room where it had all happened. As she reached this part of her narration, she pointed to the wall partitioning off the corridor, and explained that this was where the bed stood,—an old wooden one brought down from her own attic.

"'It creaked when I sat down on it,' said she, 'and I remember that I felt ashamed of its shabby mattress and the poor sheets. But we had no better,' she moaned, 'and he did not seem to mind.' I tell you this that you may understand what must have taken place in her heart when, a few minutes later, he seized her hand in his and said that he had a great secret to communicate to her. Though he had seemed the indifferent brother for years, his heart had always been with his home and his people, and he was going to prove it to her now; he had made money, and this money was to be hers and Charity's. He had saved it for them, brought it to them from the far West; a pile of money all honestly earned, which he hoped would buy back their old house and make them happy again in the old way. He said nothing of his nephew. They had not mentioned him, and possibly he did not even know of his existence. All was to be for them and the old house, this old house. This was perhaps why he was content to lie in the midst of its desolation. He foresaw better days for those he loved, and warmed his heart at his precious secret.

"But his sister sat aghast. Money! and so little done for his comfort! That was her first thought. The next, oh, the wonder and the hope of it! Now the boy could be saved; now he could have his luxuries. If only it might be enough! Five thousand, ten thousand. But no, it could not be so much. Her brother was daft to think she could restore the old home on what he had been able to save. She said something to show her doubt, at which he laughed; and, peering slowly and painfully about him, drew her hands toward his left side. 'Feel,' said he, 'I have it all here. I would trust nobody. Fifty, thousand dollars.'"

"Fifty thousand dollars! Miss Thankful sprang to her feet, then sat again, overcome by her delight. Placing her hand on the wallet he held tied about his body, she whispered, 'Here?'"

"He nodded and bade her look. She told me she did so; that she opened the wallet under his eye and took out five bonds each for ten thousand dollars. She remembers them well; there was no mistake in the figures. She held fifty thousand dollars in her hands for the space of half a minute; then he bade her put them back, with an injunction to watch over him well and not to let that woman nurse come near him till she had taken away the wallet immediately after his death. He could not bear to part with it while alive.

"She promised. She was in a delirium of joy. In one minute her life of poverty had changed to one of ecstatic hope. She caressed her brother. He smiled contentedly, and sank into coma or heavy sleep. She remained a few minutes watching him. Picture after picture of future contentment passed before her eyes; phantasmagoria of joy which held her enthralled till chance drew her eyes towards the window, and she found herself looking out upon what for the moment seemed the continuation of her dream. This was the figure of her nephew, standing in the doorway of the adjoining house. This entrance into the alley is closed up now, but in those days it was a constant source of communication between the two houses, and, being directly opposite the left-hand library window, would naturally fall under her eye as she looked up from her brother's bedside. Her nephew! the one person of whom she was dreaming, for whom she was planning, older by many years than when she saw him last, but recognizable at once, as the best, the handsomest—but I will spare you her ravings. She was certainly in her dotage as concerned this man.

"He was not alone. At his side stood her sister, eagerly pointing across the alley to herself. It was the appearance of the sister which presently convinced her that what she saw was reality and no dream. Charity had risen from her bed to greet the newcomer, and her hasty toilet was not one which could have been easily imagine, even by her sister. The long-absent one had returned. He was there, and he did not know what these last five minutes had done for them all. The joy of what she had to tell him was too much for her discretion. Noting how profoundly her brother slept, she slipped out of the room to the side door and ran across the alley to her own house. Her nephew was no longer in the doorway where she had seen him, but he had left the door ajar and she rushed in to find him. He was in the parlor with Miss Charity, and no sooner did her eyes fall on them both than her full heart overflowed, and she blurted out their good fortune. Their wonder was immense and in the conversation which ensued unnoted minutes passed. Not till the clock struck did she realize that she had left her brother alone for a good half-hour: This was not right and she went hurrying back, the happiest woman in town. But it was a short- lived happiness. As she reentered the sick-room she realized that something was amiss. Her brother had moved from where she had left him, and now lay stretched across the

Anna Katherine Green

foot of the bed, where he had evidently fallen from a standing position. He was still breathing, but in great gasps which shook the bed. When she bent over him in anxious questioning, he answered her with a ghastly stare, and that was all. Otherwise, everything looked the same.

"'What has happened? What have you done?' she persisted, trying to draw him up on the pillow. He made a motion. It was in the direction of the front door. 'Don't let her in,' he muttered. 'I don't trust her, I don't trust her. Let me die in peace.' Then, as Miss Thankful became conscious of a stir at the front door, and caught the sound of a key turning in the lock, which could only betoken the return of the nurse, he raised himself a little and she saw the wallet hanging out of his dressing gown. 'I have hidden it,' he whispered, with a nervous look toward the door: 'I was afraid she might come and take it from me, so I put it in—' He never said where. His eyes, open and staring straight before him, took on a look of horror, then slowly glazed under the terrified glance of Miss Thankful. Death had cut short that vital sentence, and simultaneously with the entrance of the nurse, whose return he had so much feared, he uttered his last gasp and sank back lifeless on his pillow. "With a cry Miss Thankful pounced on the wallet. It opened out flat in her hand, as empty as her life seemed at that minute. But she was a brave woman and in another instant her courage had revived. The money could not be far away; she would find it at the first search. Turning on the nurse, she looked her full in the face. The woman was gazing at the empty wallet. 'You know what was in that?' queried Miss Thankful. A fierce look answered her. 'A thousand dollars!' announced Miss Thankful. The nurse's lip curled. 'Oh, you knew that it was five,' was Miss Thankful's next outburst. Still no answer, but a look which seemed to devour the empty wallet. This look had its effect. Miss Thankful dropped her accusatory tone, and attempted cajolery. 'It was his legacy to us,' she explained. 'He gave it to me just before he died. You shall be paid out of it. Now will you call my sister? She's up and with my nephew, who came an hour ago. Call them both; I am not afraid to remain here for a few moments with my brother's body.' This appeal, or perhaps the promise, had its effect. The nurse disappeared, after another careful look at her patient, and Miss Thankful bounded to her feet and began a hurried search for the missing bonds. They could not be far away. They must be in the room, and the room was so nearly empty that it would take but a moment to penetrate every hiding-place. But alas! the matter was not so simple as she thought. She looked here, she looked there; in the bed, in the washstand drawer, under the cushions of the only chair, even in the grate and up the chimney; but she found nothing—nothing! She was standing stark and open- mouthed in the middle of the floor, when the others entered, but recovered herself at sight of their surprise, and, explaining what had happened, set them all to search, sister, nephew, even the nurse, though she was careful to keep close by the latter with a watchfulness that let no movement escape her. But it was all fruitless. The bonds were not to be found, either in that room or in any place near. They ransacked, they rummaged; they went upstairs, they went down; they searched every likely and every unlikely place of concealment, but without avail. They failed to come upon the place where he had hidden them; nor did Miss Thankful or her sister ever see them again from that day to this."

"Oh!" I exclaimed; "and the nephew? the nurse?"

"Both went away disappointed; he to face his disgrace about which his aunts were very reticent, and she to seek work which was all the more necessary to her, since she had lost her pay, with the disappearance of these bonds, whose value I have no doubt she knew and calculated on."

"And the aunts, the two poor old creatures who stare all day out of their upper window at these walls, still believe that money to be here," I cried.

"Yes, that is their mania. Several tenants have occupied these premises—tenants who have not stayed long, but who certainly filled all the rooms, and must have penetrated every

Anna Katherine Green

secret spot the house contains, but it has made no difference to them. They believe the bonds to be still lying in some out-of-the-way place in these old walls, and are jealous of any one who comes in here. This you can understand better when I tell you that one feature of their mania is this: they have lost all sense of time. It is two years since their brother died, yet to them it is an affair of yesterday. They showed this when they talked to me. What they wanted was for me to give up these bonds to them as soon as I found them. They seemed to think that I might run across them in settling, and made me promise to wake them day or night if I came across them unexpectedly."

"How pathetic!" I exclaimed. "Do you suppose they have appealed in the same way to every one who has come in here?"

"No, or some whisper of this lost money would have become current in the neighborhood. And it never has. The traditions associated with the house," here her manner changed a little, "are of quite another nature. I suppose the old gentleman has walked—looking, possibly, for his lost bonds."

"That would be only natural," I smiled, for her mood was far from serious. "But," I quietly pursued, "how much of this old woman's story do you believe? Can not she have been deceived as to what she saw? You say she is more or less demented. Perhaps there never was any old wallet, and possibly never any money."

"I have seen the wallet. They brought it in to show me. Not that that proves anything; but somehow I do believe in the money, and, what is more, that it is still in this house. You will think me as demented as they."

"No, no," I smiled, "for I am inclined to think the same; it lends such an interest to the place. I wouldn't disbelieve it now for anything."

"Nor I," she cried, taking up her work. "But we shall never

find it. The house was all redecorated when we came in. Not one of the workmen has become suddenly wealthy."

"I shall no longer begrudge these poor old souls their silent watch over these walls that hold their treasure," I now remarked.

"Then you have lost your nervousness?"

"Quite."

"So have I," laughed Mrs. Packard, showing me for the first time a face of complete complacency and contentment.

CHAPTER VI

AT THE STAIR-HEAD

I spent the evening alone. Mrs. Packard went to the theater with friends and Mayor Packard attended a conference of politicians. I felt my loneliness, but busied myself trying to sift the impressions made upon me by the different members of the household.

It consisted, as far as my present observation went, of seven persons, the three principals and four servants. Of the servants I had seen three, the old butler, the nurse, and the housemaid, Ellen. I now liked Ellen; she appeared equally alive and trustworthy; of the butler I could not say as much. He struck me as secretive. Also, he had begun to manifest a certain antagonism to myself. Whence sprang this antagonism? Did it have its source in my temperament, or in his? A question possibly not worth answering and yet it very well might be. Who could know?

Pondering this and other subjects, I remained in my cozy little room up-stairs, till the clock verging on to twelve told me that it was nearly time for Mrs. Packard's return.

Hardly knowing my duties as yet, or what she might expect of me, I kept my door open, meaning to speak to her when she came in. The thought had crossed my mind that she might not return at all, but remain away with her friends. Some fear of this kind had been in Mr. Packard's mind and naturally found lodgment in mine. I was therefore much relieved when, sharp on the stroke of midnight, I heard the front door-bell ring, followed by the sound of her voice speaking to the old butler. I thought its tone more cheerful than before she went out. At all events, her face had a natural look when, after a few minutes' delay, she came upstairs and stepped into the nursery—a room on the same floor as mine, but nearer the stair-head.

From what impulse did I put out my light? I think now, on looking back, that I hoped to catch a better glimpse of her face when she came out again, and so be in a position to judge whether her anxiety or secret distress was in any special way connected with her child. But I forgot the child and any motive of this kind which I may have had; for when Mrs. Packard did reappear in the hall, there rang up from some place below a laugh, so loud and derisive and of so raucous and threatening a tone that Mrs. Packard reeled with the shock and I myself was surprised in spite of my pride and usual impassibility. This, had it been all, would not be worth the comment. But it was not all. Mrs. Packard did not recover from the shock as I expected her to. Her fine figure straightened itself, it is true, but only to sink again lower and lower, till she clung crouching to the stair-rail at which she had caught for support, while her eyes, turning slowly in her head, moved till they met mine with that unseeing and glassy stare which speaks of a soul-piercing terror—not fear in any ordinary sense, but terror which lays bare the soul and allows one to see into depths which—

But here my compassion drove me to action. Advancing quietly, I caught at her wrap which was falling from her shoulders. She grasped my hand as I did so.

"Did you hear that laugh?" she panted. "Whose was it? Who is down-stairs?"

I thought, "Is this one of the unaccountable occurrences which have given the house its blighted reputation?" but I said: "Nixon let you in. I don't know whether any one else is below.

Mayor Packard has not yet come home."

"I know; Nixon told me. Would you—would you mind,"—
how hard she strove to show only the indignant curiosity
natural to the situation—"do you object, I mean, to going
down and seeing?"

"Not at all," I cheerfully answered, glad enough of this chance
to settle my own doubts. And with a last glance at her face,
which was far too white and drawn to please me, I hastened
below.

The lights had not yet been put out in the halls, though I saw
none in the drawing-room or library. Indeed, I ran upon
Nixon coming from the library, where he had evidently been
attending to his final duties of fastening windows and
extinguishing lights. Alive to the advantage of this opportune
meeting, I addressed him with as little aggressiveness as
possible.

"Mrs. Packard has sent me down to see who laughed just now
so loudly. Was it you?"

Strong and unmistakable dislike showed in his eyes, but his
voice was restrained and apparently respectful as he replied:
"No, Miss. I didn't laugh. There was nothing to laugh at."

"You heard the laugh? It seemed to come from somewhere
here. I was on the third floor and I heard it plainly."

His face twitched—a habit of his when under excitement, as I
have since learned—as with a shrug of his old shoulders he
curtly answered:

"You were listening; I was not. If any one laughed down here I
didn't hear 'em."

Confident that he was lying, I turned quietly away and
proceeded down the hall toward Mayor Packard's study.

"I wish to speak to the mayor," I explained.

"He's not there." The man had eagerly followed me. "He's not come home yet, Miss."

"But the gas is burning brightly inside and the door ajar. Some one is there."

"It is Mr. Steele. He came in an hour ago. He often works here till after midnight."

I had heard what I wanted to know, but, being by this time at the very threshold, I could not forbear giving the door a slight push, so as to catch at least a momentary glimpse of the man he spoke of.

He was sitting at his post, and as he neither looked up nor stirred at my intrusion, I had an excellent opportunity for observing again the clear-cut profile which had roused my admiration the day before.

Certainly, seen as I saw it now, in the concentrated glow of a lamp shaded from every other corner of the room, it was a face well worth looking at. Seldom, perhaps never, had I beheld one cast in a more faultless mold. Smooth-shaven, with every harmonious line open to view, it struck the eye with the force and beauty of a cameo; masculine strength and feminine grace equally expressed in the expansive forehead and the perfectly modeled features. Its effect upon the observer was instantaneous, but the heart was not warmed nor the imagination awakened by it. In spite of the perfection of the features, or possibly because of this perfection, the whole countenance had a cold look, as cold as the sculpture it suggested; and, though incomparable in pure physical attraction, it lacked the indefinable something which gives life and meaning to such faces as Mayor Packard's, for instance. Yet it was not devoid of expression, nor did it fail to possess a meaning of its own. Indeed, it was the meaning in it which held my attention. Abstracted as the man appeared to be, even to the point of not perceiving my intruding figure in the open doorway, the thoughts which held him were not common thoughts, nor were they such as could be easily read, even by an accustomed eye. Having noted this, I softly withdrew, not finding any excuse for breaking in upon a man so occupied.

The butler stood awaiting me not three feet from the door. But taking a lesson from the gentleman I had just left, I ignored his presence completely, and, tripping lightly up-stairs, found Mrs. Packard awaiting me at the head of the first flight instead of the second.

Her fears, or whatever it was which moved her, had not diminished in my absence. She stood erect, but it was by the help of her grasp on the balustrade; and though her diamonds shone and her whole appearance in her sweeping dinner-dress was almost regal, there was mortal apprehension in her eye and a passion of inquiry in her whole attitude which I was glad her husband was not there to see.

I made haste to answer that inquiry by immediately observing:

"I saw Nixon. He was just coming out of the library. He says that he heard no laugh. The only other person I came upon down-stairs was Mr. Steele. He was busy over some papers and I did not like to interrupt him; but he did not look as if a laugh of any sort had come from him."

"Thank you."

The words were hoarsely uttered and the tone unnatural, though she tried to carry it off with an indifferent gesture and a quick movement toward her room. I admired her self-control, for it was self-control, and was contrasting the stateliness of her present bearing with the cringing attitude of a few minutes before—when, without warning or any premonitory sound, all that beauty and pride and splendor collapsed before my eyes, and she fell at my feet, senseless.

CHAPTER VII

A MOVING SHADOW

I bent to lift the prostrate form of the unhappy woman who had been placed in my care. As I did so I heard something like a snarl over my shoulder, and, turning, saw Nixon stretching eager arms toward his mistress, whose fall he had doubtless heard.

"Let me! let me!" he cried, his old form trembling almost to the point of incapacity.

"We will lift her together," I rejoined; and though his eyes sparkled irefully, he accepted my help and together we carried her into her own room and laid her on a lounge. I have had some training as a nurse and, perceiving that Mrs. Packard had simply fainted, I was not at all alarmed, but simply made an effort to restore her with a calmness that for some reason greatly irritated the old man.

"Shall I call Ellen? Shall I call Letty?" he kept crying, shifting from one foot to another in a frightened and fussy way that exasperated me almost beyond endurance. "She doesn't breathe; she is white, white! Oh, what will the mayor say? I will call Letty."

But I managed to keep him under control and finally succeeded in restoring Mrs. Packard—a double task demanding not a little self-control and discretion. When the flutter of her eyelids showed that she would soon be conscious, I pointed out these signs of life to my uneasy companion and hinted very broadly that the fewer people Mrs. Packard found about her on coming to herself, the better she would be pleased. His aspect grew quite ferocious at this, and for a moment I almost feared him; but as I continued to urge the necessity of avoiding any fresh cause of agitation in one so weak, he gradually shrank back from my side where he had kept a jealous watch until now, and reluctantly withdrew into the hall.

Another moment and Mrs. Packard had started to rise; but, on seeing me and me only standing before her, she fell wearily back, crying in a subdued way, which nevertheless was very intense:

"Don't, don't let him come in—see me—or know. I must be by myself; I must be! Don't you see that I am frightened?"

The words came out with such force I was startled. Leaning over her, with the natural sympathy her condition called for, I asked quietly but firmly:

"Whom do you mean by him? There is only one person in the hall, and that is your butler."

"Hasn't Mr. Packard returned?"

"No, Madam."

"But I thought I saw him looking at me."

Her eyes were wild, her body shaking with irrepressible agitation.

"You were mistaken. Mayor Packard has not yet come home."

At this double assurance, she sank back satisfied, but still trembling and very white.

"It is Mr. Packard I meant," she whispered presently. "Stay with me and, when he comes in, tell him what will keep him from looking in or speaking to me. Promise!" She was growing wild again. "Promise, if you would be of any use to me."

"I do promise." At which I felt her hand grasp mine with grateful pressure. "Don't you wish some assistance from me? Your dress—I tried to loosen it, but failed to find the end of the cord. Shall I try again?"

"No, no; that is, I will do it myself."

I did not see how she could, for her waist was laced up the back, but I saw that she was too eager to have me go to remember this, and recognizing the undesirability of irritating her afresh, I simply asked if she wished me to remain within call.

But even this was more than she wanted.

"No. I am better now. I shall be better yet when quite alone." Then suddenly: "Who knows of this—this folly of mine?"

"Only Nixon and myself. The girls have gone to bed."

"Nixon I can trust not to speak of it. Tell him to go. You, I know, will remember only long enough to do for me what I have just asked."

"Mrs. Packard, you may trust me." The earnest, confiding look, which for a moment disturbed the melancholy of her large eyes, touched me closely as I shut the door between us.

"Now what is the meaning of this mystery?" I asked myself after I had seen Nixon go downstairs, shaking his head and casting every now and then a suspicious glance behind him. "It is not as trivial as it appears. That laugh was tragedy to her, not comedy." And when I paused to recollect its tone I did not wonder at its effect upon her mind, strained as it undoubtedly was by some secret sorrow or perplexity.

And from whose lips had that laugh sprung? Not from ghostly ones. Such an explanation I could not accept, and how could Mrs. Packard? From whose, then? If I could settle this fact I might perhaps determine to what extent its effect was dependent upon its source. The butler denied having even heard it. Was this to be believed? Did not this very denial prove that it was he and no other who had thus shocked the proprieties of this orderly household? It certainly seemed so; yet where all was strange, this strange and incomprehensible denial of a self-evident fact by the vindictive Nixon might have its source in some motive unsuggested by the circumstances. Certainly, Nixon's mistress appeared to have a great deal of confidence in him.

I wished that more had been told me about the handsome secretary. I wished that fate would give me another opportunity for seeing that gentleman and putting the same direct question to him I had put to Nixon.

Scarcely had this thought crossed my mind before a loud ring at the telephone disturbed the quiet below and I heard the secretary's voice in reply. A minute after he appeared at the foot of the stairs. His aspect was one of embarrassment, and he peered aloft in a hesitating way, as if he hardly knew how to proceed.

Taking advantage of this hesitation, I ran softly down to meet him.

"Any message for Mrs. Packard?" I asked.

He looked relieved.

"Yes, from his Honor. The mayor is unavoidably detained and may not be home till morning."

"I will tell her." Then, as he reached for his overcoat, I risked all on one venture, and enlarging a little on the facts, said:

"Excuse me, but was it you we heard laughing down-stairs a few minutes ago? Mrs. Packard feared it might be some follower of the girls'."

Pausing in the act of putting on his coat, he met my look with an air of some surprise.

"I am not given to laughing," he remarked; "certainly not when alone."

"But you heard this laugh?"

He shook his head. His manner was perfectly courteous, almost cordial.

"If I did, it made no impression on my mind. I am extremely busy just now, working up the mayor's next speech." And with a smile and bow in every way suited to his fine appearance, he took his hat from the rack and left the house.

I drew back more mystified than ever. Which of these two men had told me a lie? One, both, or neither? Impossible to determine. As I try never to waste gray matter, I resolved to spend no further energy on this question, but simply to await the next development.

It came unexpectedly and was of an entirely different nature from any I had anticipated.

I had not retired, not knowing at what moment the mayor might return or what I might be called upon to do when he did. It will be remembered that one of my windows looked out upon the next house. I approached it to see if my ever watchful neighbors had retired. Their window was dark, but I observed what was of much more vital interest to me at that moment. It was that I was not the only one awake and stirring in our house. The light from a room diagonally below me poured in a

Anna Katherine Green

stream on the opposite wall, and it took but a moment's consideration for me to decide that the shadow I saw crossing and recrossing this brilliant square was cast by Mrs. Packard.

My first impulse was to draw back—(that was the lady's impulse not quite crushed out of me by the occupation circumstances had compelled me to take up)—my next, to put out my own light and seat myself at the post of observation thus afforded me. The excuse I gave myself for this was plausible enough. Mrs. Packard had been placed in my charge and, if all was not right with her, it was my business to know it.

Accordingly I sat and watched each movement of my mysterious charge as it was outlined on the telltale wall before me, and saw enough in one half-hour to convince me that something very vigorous and purposeful was going on in the room so determinedly closed against every one, even her own husband.

What?

The moving silhouette of her figure, which was all that I could see, was not perfect enough in detail for me to determine. She was busy at some occupation which took her from one end of the room to the other; but after watching her shadow for an hour I was no surer than at first as to what that occupation was. It was a serious one, I saw, and now and then the movements I watched gave evidence of frantic haste, but their character stood unrevealed till suddenly the thought came:

"She is rummaging bureau-drawers and emptying boxes,—in other words, packing a bag or trunk."

Should I be witness to a flight? I thought it very likely, especially when I heard the faint sound of a door opening below, followed by the swish of silken skirts. I recalled Mayor Packard's fears and began to suspect that they were not groundless.

This called for action, and I was about to open my door and rush out when I was deterred by the surprising discovery that the steps I heard were coming up rather than going down, and that in another moment she would be in the hall outside, possibly on her way to the nursery, possibly with the intention of coming to my own room.

Greatly taken aback, I stood with my ear to the door, listening intently. Yes, she has reached the top of the stairs and is stopping no, she passes the nursery door, she is coming my way. What shall I say to her,—how account for my comfortable wrapper and the fact that I have not yet been abed? Had I but locked my door! Could I but lock it now, unseen and unheard before the nearing step should pause! But the very attempt were folly; no, I must stand my ground and—Ah! the step has paused, but not at my door. There is a third one on this hall, communicating, as I knew, with a covered staircase leading to the attic. It was at this she stopped and it was up this staircase she went as warily and softly as its creaking boards would allow; and while I marveled as to what had taken her aloft so late, I heard her steps over my head and knew that she had entered the room directly above mine.

Striking a match, I consulted my watch. It was just ten minutes to three. Hardly knowing what my duty was in the circumstances, I blew out the match and stood listening while the woman who was such a mystery to all her friends moved about overhead in much the same quick and purposeful way as had put life into her shadow while she was in her own room.

"Packing! Nothing less and nothing more," was my now definite decision. "That is a trunk she is dragging forward. What a hurry she is in, and how little she cares whether anybody hears her!"

So little did she care that during the next few minutes of acute attention I distinguished the flinging down of article after article on to the floor, as well as many other movements betraying haste or irritation.

Suddenly I heard her give a bound, then the sound of a heavy lid falling and then, after a minute or two of complete silence, the soft pat-pat of her slippered feet descending the stair.

Half-past three.

Waiting till she was well down the second flight, I pushed my door ajar and, flying down the hall, peered over the balustrade in time to see her entering her room. She held a lighted candle in her hand and by its small flame I caught a full glimpse of her figure. To my astonishment and even to my dismay she was still in the gown she had refused to have me unlace,—a rich yellow satin in which she must have shone resplendent a few hours before. She had not even removed the jewels from her neck. Whatever had occupied her, whatever had taken her hither and thither through the house, moving furniture out of her way, lifting heavy boxes, opening dust-covered trunks, had been of such moment to her as to make her entirely oblivious of the rich and delicate apparel she thus wantonly sacrificed. But it was not this alone which attracted my attention. In her hand she held a paper, and the sight of that paper and the way she clutched it rather disturbed my late conclusions. Had her errand been one of search rather than of arrangement? and was this crumpled letter the sole result of a half-hour's ransacking in an attic room at the dead of night? I was fain to think so, for in the course of another half-hour her light went out. Relieved that she had not left the house, I was still anxious as to the cause of her strange conduct.

Mayor Packard did not come in till daybreak. He found me waiting for him in the lower hall.

"Well?" he eagerly inquired.

"Mrs. Packard is asleep, I hope. A shrill laugh, ringing through the house shortly after her return, gave her a nervous shock and she begged that she might be left undisturbed till morning."

He turned from hanging up his overcoat, and gave me a short stare.

"A laugh!" he repeated. "Who could have laughed like that? We are not a very jolly crowd here."

"I don't know, sir. I thought it must have been either Mr. Steele or Nixon, the butler, but each denied it. There was no one else in this part of the house."

"Mrs. Packard is very sensitive just now," he remarked. Then as he turned away toward the library door: "I will throw myself on a lounge. I have but an hour or two before me, as I have my preparations to make for leaving town on the early morning train. I shall have some final instructions to give you."

CHAPTER VIII

THE PARAGRAPH

I was up betimes. Would Mrs. Packard appear at breakfast? I hardly thought so. Yet who knows? Such women have great recuperative powers, and from one so mysteriously affected anything might be expected. Ready at eight, I hastened down to the second floor to find the lady, concerning whom I had had these doubts, awaiting me on the threshold of her room. She was carefully dressed and looked pale enough to have been up for hours. An envelope was in her hand, and the smile which hailed my approach was cold and constrained.

"Good morning," said she. "Let us go down. Let us go down together. I slept wretchedly and do not feel very strong. When did Mr. Packard come in?"

"Late. He went directly to the library. He said that he had but a short time in which to rest, and would take what sleep he could get on the lounge, when I told him of your very natural nervous attack."

She sighed—a sigh which came from no inconsiderable depths—then with a proud and resolute gesture preceded me down-stairs.

Her husband was already in the breakfast-room. I could hear his voice as we turned at the foot of the stairs. Mrs. Packard, hearing it, too, drew herself up still more firmly and was passing bravely forward, when Nixon's gray head protruded from the doorway and I heard him say:

"There's company for breakfast, ma'am. His Honor could not spare Mr. Steele and asked me to set a place for him."

I noted a momentary hesitation on Mrs. Packard's part, then she silently acquiesced and we both passed on. In another instant we were receiving the greetings and apologies of the gentlemen. If Mr. Steele had expected that his employer's wife would offer him her hand, he was disappointed.

"I am happy to welcome one who has proved so useful to my husband," she remarked with cool though careful courtesy as we all sat down at the table; and, without waiting for an answer, she proceeded to pour the coffee with a proud grace which gave no hint of the extreme feeling by which I had seen her moved the night before.

Had I known her better I might have found something extremely unnatural in her manner and the very evident restraint she put upon herself through the whole meal; but not having any acquaintance with her ordinary bearing under conditions purely social, I was thrown out of my calculations by the cold ease with which she presided at her end of the table, and the set smile with which she greeted all remarks, whether volunteered by her husband or by his respectful but affable secretary. I noticed, however, that she ate little.

Nixon, whom I dared not watch, did not serve with his usual precision,—this I perceived from the surprised look cast at him by Mayor Packard on at least two occasions. Though to the ordinary eye a commonplace meal, it had elements of tragedy in it which made the least movement on the part of those engaged in it of real moment to me. I was about to leave the table unenlightened, however, when Mrs. Packard rose and, drawing a letter from under the tray before which she sat, let her glances pass from one gentleman to the other with a look of decided inquiry. I drew in my breath and by dropping my handkerchief sought an excuse for lingering in the room an instant longer.

"Will—may I ask one of you," she stammered with her first show of embarrassment during the meal, "to—to post this letter for me?"

Both gentlemen were standing and both gentlemen reached for it; but it was into the secretary's hand she put it, though her husband's was much the nearer. As Mr. Steele received it he gave it the casual glance natural under the circumstances,—a glance which instantly, however, took on an air of surprise that ended in a smile.

"Have you not made some mistake?" he asked.

"This does not look like a letter." And he handed her back the paper she had given him. With an involuntary ingathering of her breath, she seemed to wake out of some dream and, looking down at the envelope she held, she crushed it in her hand with a little laugh in which I heard the note of real gaiety for the first time.

"Pardon me," she exclaimed; and, meeting his amused gaze with one equally expressive, she carelessly added: "I certainly brought a letter down with me."

Bowing pleasantly, but with that indefinable air of respect which bespeaks the stranger, he waited while she hastened back to the tray and drew from under it a second paper.

"Pardon my carelessness," she said. "I must have caught up a scrawl of the baby's in taking this from my desk."

She brought forward a letter and ended the whole remarkable episode by handing it now to her husband, who, with an apologetic glance at the other, put it in his pocket.

I say remarkable; for in the folded slip which had passed back and forth between her and the secretary, I saw, or thought I saw, a likeness to the paper she had brought the night before out of the attic.

If Mayor Packard saw anything unusual in his wife's action he made no mention of it when I went into his study at nine o'clock. And it was so much of an enigma to me that I was not ready to venture a question regarding it.

Her increased spirits and more natural conduct were the theme of the few sentences he addressed me, and while he urged precaution and a continued watch upon his wife, he expressed the fondest hope that he should find her fully restored on his return at the end of two weeks.

I encouraged his hopes, and possibly shared them; but I changed my mind, as he probably did his, when a few minutes later we met her in the hall hurrying toward us with a newspaper in her hand and a ghastly look on her face. "See! see! what they have dared to print!" she cried, with a look, full of anguish, into his bewildered face.

He took the sheet, read, and flushed, then suddenly grew white. "Outrageous!" he exclaimed. Then tenderly, "My poor darling! that they should dare to drag your name into this abominable campaign!"

"And for no reason," she faltered; "there is nothing wrong with me. You believe that; you are sure of that," she cried. I saw the article later. It ran something like this:

"Rumor has it that not even our genial mayor's closet is free from the proverbial skeleton. Mrs. Packard's health is not what it was,—and some say that the causes are not purely physical."

He tried to dissimulate. Putting his arm about her, he kissed her fondly and protested with mingled energy and feeling:

"I believe you to be all you should be—a true woman and

Anna Katherine Green

true wife."

Her face lighted and she clung for a moment in passionate delight to his breast; then she caught his look, which was tender but not altogether open, and the shadows fell again as she murmured:

"You are not satisfied. Oh, what do you see, what do others see, that I should be the subject of doubt? Tell me! I can never right myself till I know."

"I see a troubled face when I should see a happy one," he answered lightly; then, as she still clung in very evident question to his arm, he observed gravely: "Two weeks ago you were the life of this house, and of every other house into which your duties carried you. Why shouldn't you be the same to-day? Answer me that, dear, and all my doubts will vanish, I assure you."

"Henry,"—drooping her head and lacing her fingers in and out with nervous hesitation,—"you will think me very foolish,—I know that it will sound foolish, childish even, and utterly ridiculous; but I can explain myself no other way. I have had a frightful experience—here—in my own house—on the spot where I have been so happy, so unthinkingly happy. Henry—do not laugh—it is real, very real, to me. The specter which is said to haunt these walls has revealed itself to me. I have seen the ghost."

CHAPTER IX

SCRAPS

We did not laugh; we did not even question her sanity; at least I did not; there was too much meaning in her manner.

"A specter," her husband repeated with a suggestive glance at the brilliant sunshine in which we all stood.

"Yes." The tone was one of utter conviction. "I had never believed in such things—never thought about them, but—it was a week ago—in the library—I have not seen a happy moment since—"

"My darling!"

"Yes, yes, I know; but imagine! I was sitting reading. I had just come from the nursery, and the memory of Laura's good-night kiss was more in my mind than the story I was finishing when—oh, I can not think of it without a shudder!—the page before me seemed to recede and the words fade away in a blue mist; glancing up I beheld the outlines of a form between me and the lamp. which a moment before had been burning brightly. Outlines, Henry,—I was conscious of no substance, and the eyes which met mine from that shadowy, blood-curdling Something were those of the grave and meant a grave for you or for me. Oh, I know what I say! There was no mistaking their look. As it burned into and through me, everything which had given reality to my life faded and seemed

Anna Katherine Green

as far away and as unsubstantial as a dream. Nor has its power over me gone yet. I go about amongst you, I eat, I sleep, or try to; I greet men, talk with women, but it is all unreal, all phantasmagoric, even yourself and your love and, O God, my baby! What is real and distinctive, an absolute part of me and my life, is that shape from the dead, with its threatening eyes which pierce—pierce—"

She was losing her self-control. Her husband, with a soothing touch on her arm, brought her back to the present.

"You speak of a form," he said, "a shadowy outline. The form of what? A man or a woman?"

"A man! a man!" With the exclamation she seemed to shrink into herself and her eyes, just now deprecating and appealing, took on a hollow stare, as if the vision she described had risen again before her.

In spite of himself and the sympathy he undoubtedly felt for her, an ejaculation of impatience left her husband's lips. Obligations very far removed from the fantasies of a disturbed mind made these unsubstantial fears of hers seem puerile enough to this virile, outspoken man. No doubt she heard it, and to stop the matter-of- fact protest on his lips added quickly:

"Not the form, face and eyes of a man, as they usually appear. Hell was in his gaze and the message he gave, if it was a message, was one of disaster, if not death. Do you wonder that my happiness vanished before it? That I can not be myself since that dreadful day?"

The mayor was a practical man; he kept close to the subject.

"You saw this form between you and the lighted lamp. How long did it stay there and what became of it?"

"I can not tell you. One moment it was there and the next it was gone, and I found myself staring into vacancy. I seem to be staring there still, waiting for the blow destined to shatter this household."

"Nonsense! give me a kiss and fix your thoughts on something more substantial. What we have to fear and all we have to fear is that I may lose my election. And that won't kill me, whatever effect it may have on the party."

"Henry,"—her voice had changed to one more natural, also her manner. The confidence expressed in this outburst, the vitality, the masculine attitude he took were producing their effect. "You don't believe in what I saw or in my fears. Perhaps you are right. I am ready to acknowledge this; I will try to look upon it all as a freak of my imagination if you will promise to forget these dreadful days, and if people, other people, will leave me alone and not print such things about me."

"I am ready to do my part," was his glad reply, "and as for the other people you mention, we shall soon bring them to book." Raising his voice, he called out his secretary's name. As it rang loud and cheery down the hall, the joy and renewed life which had been visible in her manner lost some of their brightness.

"What are you going to do?" she gasped, with the quickness of doubt and strong if reasonless apprehension. "Give an order," he explained; then, as the secretary appeared at our end of the hall, he held out the journal which he had taken from his wife and indicating the offensive paragraph, said:

"Find out who did that."

Mr. Steele with a surprised look ran his eyes over the paragraph, knitting his brows as he did.

"It is calumny," fell from Mrs. Packard's lips as she watched him.

"Most certainly," he assented, with an energy which brought a flush of pleasure to the humiliated woman's cheek. "It will detain me two days or more to follow up this matter," he remarked, with a look of inquiry directed at Mayor Packard.

"Never mind. Two days or a week, it is all one. I would rather lose votes than pass over such an insult. Pin me down the man who has dared attack me through my wife, and you will do me the greatest favor one man can show another."

Mr. Steele bowed. "I can not forego the final consultation we had planned to hold on the train. May I ride down with you to the station?"

"Certainly; most happy."

Mr. Steele withdrew, after casting a glance of entirely respectful sympathy at the woman who up to this hour had faced the world without a shadow between her and it; and, marking the lingering nature of the look with which the mayor now turned on his wife, I followed the secretary's example and left them to enjoy their few last words alone.

Verily the pendulum of events swung wide and fast in this house.

This conclusion was brought back to me with fresh insistence a few minutes later, when, on hearing the front door shut, I stepped to the balustrade and looked over to see if Mrs. Packard was coming up. She was not, for I saw her go into the library; but plainly on the marble pavement below, just where we had all been standing, in fact, I perceived the piece of paper she had brought with her from the dining-room and had doubtless dropped in the course of the foregoing conversation.

Running down in great haste, I picked it up. This scrap of I knew not what, but which had been the occasion of the enigmatic scene I had witnessed at the breakfast-table, necessarily interested me very much and I could not help giving it a look. I saw that it was inscribed with Hebraic-looking characters as unlike as possible to the scrawl of a little child.

With no means of knowing whether they were legible or not, these characters made a surprising impression upon me, one, indeed, that was almost photographic.

I also noted that these shapes or characters, of which there were just seven, were written on the face of an empty envelope. This decided any doubts I may have had as to its identity with the paper she had brought down from the attic. That had been a square sheet, which even if folded would fail to enter this long and narrow envelope. The interest which I had felt when I thought the two identical was a false interest. Yet I could not but believe that this scrap had a value of its own equal to the one with which, under this misapprehension, I had invested it.

Carrying it back to Mrs. Packard, I handed it over with the remark that I had found it lying in the hall. She cast a quick look at it, gave me another look and tossed the paper into the grate. As it caught fire and flared up, the characters started vividly into view.

This second glimpse of them, added to the one already given me, fixed the whole indelibly in my mind. This is the way they looked.

[]; V; []; .>; V; [-]; <;

While I watched these cabalistic marks pass from red to black and finally vanish in a wild leap up the chimney, Mrs. Packard remarked:

"I wish I could destroy the memory of all my mistakes as completely as I can that old envelope."

I did not answer; I was watching the weary droop of her hand over the arm of her chair.

"You are tired, Mrs. Packard," was my sympathetic observation. "Will you not take a nap? I will gladly sit by you and read you to sleep."

"No, no," she cried, at once alert and active; "no sleep. Look at that pile of correspondence, half of it on charitable matters. Now that I feel better, now that I have relieved my mind, I must look over my letters and try to take up the old threads again."

"Can I help you?" I asked.

"Possibly. If you will go to my room up-stairs, I will join you after I have sorted and read my mail."

I was glad to obey this order. I had a curiosity about her room. It had been the scene of much I did not understand the night before. Should I find any traces there of that search which had finally ended over my head in the attic?

I was met at the door by Ellen. She wore a look of dismay which I felt fully accounted for when I looked inside. Disorder reigned from one end of the room to the other, transcending any picture I may have formed in my own mind concerning its probable condition. Mrs. Packard must have forgotten all this disarray, or at least had supposed it to have yielded to the efforts of the maid, when she proposed my awaiting her there. There were bureau-drawers with their contents half on the floor, boxes with their covers off, cupboard-doors ajar and even the closet shelves showing every mark of a frenzied search among them. Her rich gown, soiled to the width of half a foot around the bottom, lay with cut laces and its trimmings in rags under a chair which had been knocked over and left where it fell. Even her jewels had not been put away, but lay scattered on the dresser. Ellen looked ashamed and, when I retired to the one bare place I saw in the bay of the window, muttered as she plunged to lift one of the great boxes:

"It's as bad as the attic room up-stairs. All the trunks have been emptied on to the floor and one held her best summer dresses. What shall I do? I have a whole morning's work before me."

"Let me help you," I proposed, rising with sudden alacrity. My eyes had just fallen on a small desk at my right, also on the floor beneath and around it. Here, there and everywhere above and below lay scraps of torn-up paper; and on many, if not on all of them, could be seen the broken squares and inverted angles which had marked so curiously the surface of the envelope she had handed to Mr. Steele, and which I had afterward seen her burn.

"A baby can make a deal of mess," I remarked, hurriedly collecting these scraps and making a motion of throwing them into the waste- paper basket, but hiding them in my blouse instead.

"The baby! Oh, the baby never did that. She's too young."

"Oh, I didn't know. I haven't seen much of the child though I heard her cry once in the nursery. How old is she?"

"Twenty months and such a darling! You never saw such curls or such eyes. Why, look at this!"

"What?" I demanded, hurrying to the closet, where Ellen stood bending over something invisible to me. "Oh, nothing," she answered, coming quickly out. But in another moment, her tongue getting the better of her discretion, she blurted out: "Do you suppose Mrs. Packard had any idea of going with the mayor? Her bag is in there almost packed. I was wondering where all her toilet articles were. That accounts—" Stopping, she cast a glance around the room, ending with a shake of the head and a shrug. "She needn't have pulled out all her things," she sharply complained. "Certain, she is a mysterious lady;—as queer as she is kind."

CHAPTER X

A GLIMMER OF THE TRUTH

This was a sentiment I could thoroughly indorse. Mrs. Packard was certainly an enigma to me. Leaving Ellen to finish her work, I went upstairs to my own room, and, taking out the scraps of paper I had so carefully collected, spread them out before me on the lid of the desk.

They were absolutely unintelligible to me—marks and nothing more. Useless to waste time over such unmeaning scrawls when I had other and more tangible subjects to consider. But I should not destroy them. There might come a time when I should be glad to give them the attention which my present excitement forbade. Putting them back in my desk, I settled myself into a serious contemplation of the one fact which seemed to give a partial if not wholly satisfactory explanation of Mrs. Packard's peculiar conduct during the last two weeks—her belief that she had been visited by a specter of an unholy, threatening aspect.

That it was a belief and nothing more seemed sufficiently clear to me in the cold-blooded analysis to which I now subjected the whole matter.

Phantoms have no place in the economy of nature. That Mrs. Packard thought herself the victim of one was simply a proof of how deeply, though perhaps unconsciously, she had been affected by the traditions of the house. Such sensitiveness in a mind naturally firm and uncommonly well poised, called for attention. Yet a physician had asserted that he could do nothing for her. Granting that he was mistaken, would an interference of so direct and unmistakable a character be wise in the present highly strung condition of her nerves? I doubted it. It would show too plainly the light in which we regarded her. I dared not undertake the responsibility of such a course in Mayor Packard's absence. Some other way must be found to quiet her apprehensions and bring her into harmony again with her surroundings. I knew of only one course. If the influence of the house had brought on this hallucination, then the influence of the house must be destroyed. She must be made to see that, despite its unfortunate reputation, no specter had ever visited it; that some purely natural cause was at the bottom of the various manifestations which had successively driven away all previous tenants.

Could I hope to effect this? It was an undertaking of no small moment. Had I the necessary judgment? I doubted it, but my ambition was roused. While Mr. Steele was devoting himself to the discovery of Mayor and Mrs. Packard's political enemy, I would essay the more difficult task of penetrating the mystery threatening their domestic peace. I could but fail; a few inquiries would assure me of the folly or the wisdom of my course.

Having reached this point and satisfied myself as to my real duty, I rose to leave my room for another word or two with Ellen. As I did so my eyes fell on the shade still drawn between me and the next house. The impulse to raise it was irresistible. I must see if either of the two old faces still occupied that gable window. It was not likely. It was not in ordinary human nature to keep up so unremitting a watch. Yet as the shade flew up at my touch I realized that my astonishment would have been great and my expectations altogether disappointed if I had not encountered the fixed countenance and the set stare with which I had come to connect this solitary window. Miss Charity was there, and, though I now knew what underlay her senile, if not utterly mad watch, the impression made upon me

Anna Katherine Green

by her hopeless countenance was as keen as it had ever been, and lent point and impetus to the task I had just set for myself.

It was apparent that Mrs. Packard had forgotten or changed her mind about joining me in her own room, but nevertheless I went out, to discover what possible duties she might have laid out for me. Ascertaining from Ellen that Mrs. Packard had engagements which would take her out at noon, I waited for that hour to pass, then excused myself and went out also.

The owner of the house whose shaded history I was now determined to learn was John Searles, a real estate agent. To his office in Main Street I at once proceeded, not without doubts and much inward trepidation, but buoyed up by the assurance of Mayor Packard's approval of any attempt, however far-fetched or unpromising, which held out the least possibility of relieving Mrs. Packard from her superstitious fears and restoring the peace and happiness of the household. If only Mr. Searles should prove to be an approachable man!

I had never seen him or heard him spoken of, or I should not have encouraged myself with this hope. At my first glimpse of his tall, gaunt figure, hard features, and brisk impatient movements, I knew that my wit and equanimity would be put to their full test in the interview.

He was engaged, at my entrance, in some harsh dispute with a couple of other men, but came forward quickly enough when he saw me. Recognizing at once that any attempt at ingratiation would fail with this man, I entered at once upon my errand by asking a question direct enough to command his attention, if it did not insure the desired reply.

"Mr. Searles, when you purchased the house on Franklin Street, did you know enough about it to have an answer ready for any one who might declare it haunted?"

The abruptness of the attack produced its effect. Annoyance swept every hint of patience from face and manner, and he exclaimed in a tone which conveyed, only too openly, how disagreeable the subject was to him.

"Again!"

I smiled. It would not do to show how much I felt the total lack of sympathy in his manner.

"You will have trouble," said I, "until it is proved that the occurrences which have provoked this report have a very natural and quite human source."

He stopped in his nervous fidgeting and gave me a quick hard look.

"Who are you?" he asked, "and why has Mrs. Packard made you her messenger instead of coming herself?"

"I am her companion, engaged by Mayor Packard to stay with her during his contemplated absence. I am here instead of Mrs. Packard because it is she herself who is the present sufferer from the disagreeable experiences which attend life in the Franklin Street house."

"Mrs. Packard?" His tone betrayed a complete incredulity. "Mrs. Packard? a woman of such strong good sense! I think you must have been misled by some foolish attempt at humor on her part. Does she know that you have come to me with this complaint?"

"She does not. She is not in a condition to be consulted on the subject. I am Mayor Packard's emissary. He is very anxious about his wife." Then as Mr. Searles continued unmoved, I added in a straightforward manner, and with all the earnestness I felt: "Mrs. Packard believes herself to have come face to face with an undoubted specter in the library of the house they have rented from you. She related the circumstances to her husband and to myself this very morning. It occurred, according to her story, several days ago; meantime her manner and appearance have shown a great change. Mayor Packard is not the only one who has noticed it. The whole household has been struck by her condition, though no one knew its cause until to-day. Of course, we do not believe in the specter; that was pure hallucination on her part. This we no more doubt than you do."

"Then what do you want here?" he asked, after a moment of harsh scrutiny.

"Proof which will convince her that it was an hallucination and without the least basis in any spiritual fact," I returned. "If you will give me a few minutes of your time, I will explain just what I mean and also make known to you my wishes. I can wait till you have finished your business with the gentlemen I see over there."

He honored me with a look, which for the first time showed any appreciation of my feelings, and pushing open a door near by, called out to some one within:

"Here, Robinson, talk with this lady. Her business is not in my line." Then, turning to me with a quick, "Step in, Madam," he left me with the greatest abruptness and hurried back to the gentlemen awaiting him on the other side of the room.

I was considerably taken aback by this move, but knew no other course than to enter the room he had pointed out and pursue my conversation with whomever I should find there.

Alas! the gentleman who rose at my entrance was also one of the tall, thin and nervous type. But he was not without heart, like the other, as was soon made apparent to me. Very few human faces are plainer than the one I now searched for the encouragement of which I stood in such sore need, but also very few faces, handsome or otherwise, have the attraction of so pleasant a smile. Its affable greeting was followed by the hasty pushing forward of a chair and a kind inquiry as to what he could do for me.

My answer woke an immediate interest. "My name is Saunders," I said. "I am at present an inmate of Mayor Packard's house—a house belonging to Mr. Searles, and one which has its drawbacks."

The meaning look with which I uttered the last sentence called forth an answering one. A flash of excitement broke over his features and he cast a quick glance at the door which fortunately had swung to at my entrance.

"Has—have they—has anything of a disagreeable nature happened to any one in this house?" he asked with ill-concealed perturbation. "I did not expect it during their tenantry, but if such has occurred, I am obliged to Mrs. Packard for letting me know. She promised to, you see, and—"

"She promised!" I cried.

"Yes; in joke no doubt, being at the time in a very incredulous state of mind. She vowed that she would let me know the very day she saw the lights or encountered anything in the house, which could be construed into a spiritual visitation. Has such a manifestation occurred?" he eagerly inquired. "Has it? has it? Am I to add her name to the list of those who have found the house uninhabitable?"

"That I am not ready to say," was my cautious response. "Mrs. Packard, during the period of her husband's candidacy, would scarcely wish to draw public attention to herself or these supernatural happenings by any such move. I hope that what I say to you on this subject will go no further."

"You may rest assured that it will never become public property," he assured me. "One person I am bound to tell; but that is all. That person is too much interested in the house's good name to spread so damaging a story. An experience, more or less disagreeable, must have occurred to some member of the family," continued Mr. Robinson. "Your presence here assures me of that. What kind of experience?

The—manifestations have not always been of the same nature."

"No; and that is what so engages my attention. These experiences differ so much in their character. Do you happen to know the exact nature of each? I have a theory which I long to substantiate. May I trust you with it?"

"You certainly may, Miss. No one has thought over this matter more earnestly than I have. Not because of any superstitious tendency on my part; rather from the lack of it. I don't believe in spirits. I don't believe in supernatural agencies of any kind; yet strange things do happen in that house, things which we find it hard to explain."

"Mrs. Packard's experience was this. She believes herself to have encountered in the library the specter of a man; a specter with a gaze so terrifying that it impressed itself upon her as an omen of death, or some other dire disaster. What have your other tenants seen?"

"Shadows mostly; but not always. Sometimes the outline of an arm projecting out of darkness; sometimes, the trace of steps on the hall floors, or the discovery in the morning of an open door which had been carefully closed at bedtime. Once it was the trailing of ghostly fingers across the sleeper's face, and once a succession of groans rising from the lower halls and drawing the whole family from their beds, to find no one but themselves within the whole four walls. A clearly outlined phantom has been scarce. But Mrs. Packard has seen one, you say."

"Thinks she has seen one," I corrected. "Mayor Packard and myself both look upon the occurrence as a wholly imaginary one, caused by her secret brooding over the very manifestations you mention. If she could be convinced that these manifestations had a physical origin, she would immediately question the reality of the specter she now believes herself to have seen. To bring her to this point I am ready to exert myself to the utmost. Are you willing to do the same? If so, I can assure you of Mayor Packard's appreciation."

"How? What? You believe the whole thing a fraud? That all these tenants coming from various quarters manufactured all these stories and submitted to endless inconvenience to perpetuate a senseless lie?"

"No, I don't think that. The tenants were honest enough, but who owned the house before Mr. Searles?" I was resolved to give no hint of the information imparted to me by Mrs. Packard.

"The Misses Quinlan, the two maiden ladies who live next door to Mayor Packard."

"I don't know them," said I truthfully.

"Very worthy women," Mr. Robinson assured me. "They are as much disturbed and as completely puzzled as the rest of us over the mysterious visitations which have lessened the value of their former property. They have asked me more than once for an explanation of its marked unpopularity. I felt foolish to say ghosts, but finally I found myself forced to do so, much to my lasting regret."

"How? Why?" I asked, with all the force of a very rapidly increasing curiosity.

"Because its effect upon them has been so disastrous. They were women of intelligence previous to this, one of them quite markedly so, but from that day they have given evidence of mental weakness which can only be attributed to their continual brooding over this mysterious topic. The house, whose peculiarities we are now discussing, was once their family homestead, and they shrink from the reproach of its unfortunate reputation. What! you don't think so?" he impetuously asked, moved, perhaps, by my suggestive silence. "You are suspicious of these two poor old women? What reason have you for that, Miss Saunders? What motive could they have for depreciating the value of what was once their own property?"

So he knew nothing of the lost bonds! Mrs. Packard had made no mistake when she assured me of the secrecy with which they had endured their misfortune. It gave me great relief; I could work more safely with this secret unshared. But the situation called for dissimulation. It was with anything but real openness that I declared:

"You can not calculate the impulses of an affected mind. Jealousy of the past may influence these unfortunate women. They possibly hate to see strangers in the rooms made sacred by old associations."

"That is possible, but how could they, shut up in a house, separated from yours by a distance of several feet, be held accountable for the phenomena observed in 393? There are no means of communication between the two buildings; even the doors, which once faced each other across the dividing alley, have been closed up. Interference from them is impossible."

"No more impossible than from any other outside source. Is it a fact that the doors and windows of this strangely haunted house were always found securely locked after each occurrence of the phenomena you have mentioned?"

"So I have been told by every tenant I have questioned, and I was careful to question them, I assure you."

"That settles the matter in my mind," I asserted. "These women know of some means of entrance that has escaped general discovery. Cunning is a common attribute of the unsettled brain."

"And they are very cunning. Miss Saunders, you have put a totally new idea into my head. I do not place much stress upon the motive you have attributed to them, nor do I see how the appearances noted could have been produced by these two antiquated women; but the interest they have displayed in the effect these have had upon others has been of the most decided nature. They have called here after the departure of every fresh tenant, and it was all that I could do to answer their persistent inquiries. It is to them and not to Mr. Searles I feel bound to report the apparition seen by Mrs. Packard."

"To them!" I ejaculated in amazement. "Why to them? They no longer have a proprietary interest in the house."

"Very true, but they long ago exacted a promise from me to keep a strict account of such complaints as were raised against the house. They, in short, paid me to do so. From time to time they have come here to read this account. It annoys Mr. Searles, but I have had considerable patience with them for reasons which your kind heart will instantly suggest."

I thought of the real pathos of the situation, and how much I might increase his interest by giving him the full details of their pitiful history, and the maddening hopes it engendered of a possible discovery of the treasure they still believed to be hidden in the house. What I said, however, was this:

"You have kept an account, you say, of the varied phenomena seen in this house? You have that account now?"

"Yes, Miss Saunders."

"Let us look it over together. Let us see if it does not give us some clue to the mystery puzzling us."

He eyed me doubtfully, or as much so as his great nature would allow. Meantime, I gauged my man. Was he to be thoroughly and unequivocally trusted? His very hesitation in face of his undoubted sympathy with me seemed to insure that he was. At all events, the occasion warranted some risk on my part. At least I persuaded myself that it did; so without waiting for his reply, I earnestly remarked:

Anna Katherine Green

"The matter is more serious than you suppose. If the mayor were not unavoidably called away by his political obligations, he would add his entreaties to mine for a complete sifting of this whole affair. The Misses Quinlan may very well be innocent of inciting these manifestations; if so, we can do them no harm by a little confidential consideration of the affair from the standpoint I have given you. If they are not, then Mr. Searles and Mayor Packard should know it."

It appeared to convince him. His homely face shone with the fire of sudden interest and resolve, and, reaching for a small drawer at the right of his desk, he opened it and drew forth a folded paper which he proceeded to open before me with the remark:

"Here is a report that I have kept for my own satisfaction. I do not feel that in showing it to you I am violating any trust reposed in me by the Misses Quinlan. I never promised secrecy in the matter."

I glanced at the paper, all eagerness. He smiled and pushed it toward me. This is what I read:

First tenant, Mr. Hugh Dennison and family.

Night 1: Heard and saw nothing.
Night 2: The entire household wakened by a scream seemingly coming from below. This was twice repeated before Mr. Dennison could reach the hall; the last time in far distant and smothered tones. Investigation revealed nothing. No person and no trace of any persons, save themselves, could be found anywhere in the house. Uncomfortable feelings, but no alarm as yet.
Night 3: No screams, but a sound of groaning in the library. The tall clock standing near the drawing-room door stopped at twelve, and a door was found open which Mr. Dennison is sure he shut tight on retiring. A second unavailing search. One servant left the next morning.
Night 4: Footfalls on the stairs. The library door, locked by

Mr. Dennison's own hand, is heard to unclose. The timepiece on the library mantel-shelf strikes twelve; but it is slightly fast, and Mr. and Mrs. Dennison, who have crept from their room to the stair-head, listen breathlessly for the deep boom of the great hall clock—the one which had stopped the night before. No light is burning anywhere, and the hall below is a pit of darkness, when suddenly Mrs. Dennison seizes her husband's arm and, gasping out, "The clock, the clock!" falls fainting to the floor. He bends to look and faintly, in the heart of the shadows, he catches in dim outline the face of the clock, and reaching up to it a spectral hand. Nothing else—and in another moment that, too, disappears; but the silence is something awful—the great clock has stopped. With a shout he stumbles downward, lights up the hall, lights up the rooms, but finds nothing, and no one. Next morning the second servant leaves, but her place is soon supplied by an applicant we will call Bess.

Night 5: Mrs. Dennison sleeps at a hotel with the children. Mr. Dennison, revolver in hand, keeps watch on the haunted stairway. He has fastened up every door and shutter with his own hand, and with equal care extinguished all lights. As the hour of twelve approaches, he listens breathlessly. There is certainly a stir somewhere, but he can not locate it, not quite satisfy himself whether it is a footfall or a rustle that he hears. The clock in the library strikes twelve, then the one in the hall gives one great boom, and stops. Instantly he raises his revolver and shoots directly at its face. No sound from human lips answers the discharge of the weapon. In the flash which for a moment has lighted up the whole place, he catches one glimpse of the broken dial with its two hands pointing directly at twelve, but nothing more. Then all is dark again, and he goes slowly back to his own room. The next day he threw up his lease.

Second tenant: Mrs. Crispin.

Stayed but one night. Would never tell us what she saw.

Anna Katherine Green

Third tenant: Mrs. Southwick. Hires Bess for maid-of-all-work, the only girl she could get.

Night 1: Unearthly lights shining up through the house, waking the family. Disappeared as one and all came creeping out into the hall.
Night 2: The same, followed by deep groans. Children waked and shrieked.
Night 3: Nothing.
Night 4: Lights, groans and strange shadows on the walls and ceilings of the various hallways. Family give notice the next day, but do not leave for a week, owing to sickness. No manifestations while doctor and nurses are in the house.

House stands vacant for three months. Bess offers to remain in it as caretaker, but her offer is refused.

Police investigate.

An amusing farce. One of them saw something and could not be laughed out of it by his fellows. But the general report was unsatisfactory. The mistake was the employment of Irishmen in a task involving superstition.

Fourth tenant: Mr. Weston and family.

Remain three weeks. Leaves suddenly because the nurse encountered something moving about in the lower hall one night when she went down to the kitchen to procure hot water for a sick child. Bess again offered her services, but the family would not stay under any circumstances.

Another long period without tenant.

Mr. Searles tries a night in the empty house. Sits and dozes in library till two. Wakes suddenly. Door he has tightly shut is standing open. He feels the draft. Turns on light from dark lantern. Something is there—a shape—he can not otherwise describe it. As he stares at it, it vanishes through doorway. He rushes for it; finds nothing. The hall is empty; so is the whole house.

This finished the report.

"So Mr. Searles has had his own experiences of these Mysteries!" I exclaimed.

"As you see. Perhaps that is why he is so touchy on the subject."

"Did he ever give you any fuller account of his experience than is detailed here?"

"No; he won't talk about it."

"He tried to let the house, however."

"Yes, but he did not succeed for a long time. Finally the mayor took it."

Refolding the paper, I handed it back to Mr. Robinson. I had its contents well in mind.

"There is one fact to which I should like to call your attention," said I. "The manifestations, as here recorded, have all taken place in the lower part of the house. I should have had more faith in them, if they had occurred above stairs. There are no outlets through the roof."

"Nor any visible ones below. At least no visible one was ever found open."

"What about the woman, Bess?" I asked. "How do you account for her persistency in clinging to a place her employers invariably fled from? She seems to have been always on hand with an offer of her services."

"Bess is not a young woman, but she is a worker of uncommon ability, very rigid and very stoical. She herself accounts for her willingness to work in this house by her utter disbelief in spirits, and the fact that it is the one place in the world which connects her with her wandering and worthless husband. Their final parting occurred during Mr. Dennison's tenancy, and as she had given the wanderer the Franklin Street address, you could not reason her out of the belief that on his return he would expect to find here there. That is what she explained to Mr. Searles."

"You interest me, Mr. Robinson. Is she a plain woman? Such a one as a man would not be likely to return to?"

"No, she is a very good-looking woman, refined and full of character, but odd, very odd,—in fact, baffling."

"How baffling?"

"I never knew her to look any one directly in the eye. Her manner is abstracted and inspires distrust. There is also a marked incongruity between her employment and her general appearance. She looks out of place in her working apron, yet she is not what you would call a lady."

"Did her husband come back?"

"No, not to my knowledge."

"And where is she now?"

"Very near you, Miss Saunders, when you are at your home in Franklin Street. Not being able to obtain a situation in the house itself, she has rented the little shop opposite, where you can find her any day selling needles and thread."

"I have noticed that shop," I admitted, not knowing whether to give more or less weight to my suspicions in thus finding the mayor's house under the continued gaze of another watchful eye.

"You will find two women there," the amiable Mr. Robinson hastened to explain. "The one with a dark red spot just under her hair is Bess. But perhaps she doesn't interest you. She always has me. If it had not been for one fact, I should have suspected her of having been in some way connected with the strange doings we have just been considering. She was not a member of the household during the occupancy of Mrs. Crispin and the Westons, yet these unusual manifestations went on just the same."

"Yes, I noted that."

"So her connivance is eliminated."

"Undoubtedly. I am still disposed to credit the Misses Quinlan with the whole ridiculous business. They could not bear to see strangers in the house they had once called their own, and took the only means suggested to their crazy old minds to rid the place of them."

Mr. Robinson shook his head, evidently unconvinced. The temptation was great to strengthen my side of the argument by a revelation of their real motive. Once acquainted with the story of the missing bonds he could not fail to see the extreme probability that the two sisters, afflicted as they were with dementia, should wish to protect the wealth which was once so near their grasp, from the possibility of discovery by a stranger. But I dared not take him quite yet into my full confidence. Indeed, the situation did not demand it. I had learned from him what I was most anxious to know, and was now in a position to forward my own projects without further aid from him. Almost as if he had read my thoughts, Mr. Robinson now hastened to remark:

"I find it difficult to credit these poor old souls with any such elaborate plan to empty the house, even had they possessed the most direct means of doing so, for no better reason than this

Anna Katherine Green

one you state. Had money been somehow involved, or had they even thought so, it would be different. They are a little touched in the head on the subject of money; which isn't very strange considering their present straits. They even show an interest in other people's money. They have asked me more than once if any of their former neighbors have seemed to grow more prosperous since leaving Franklin Street."

"I see; touched, touched!" I laughed, rising in my anxiety to hide any show of feeling at the directness of this purely accidental attack. But the item struck me as an important one. Mr. Robinson gave me a keen look as I uttered the usual commonplaces and prepared to take my leave.

"May I ask your intentions in this matter?" said he.

"I wish I knew them myself," was my perfectly candid answer. "It strikes me now that my first step should be to ascertain whether there exists any secret connection between the two houses which would enable the Misses Quinlan or their emissaries to gain access to their old home, without ready detection. I know of none, and—"

"There is none," broke in its now emphatic agent. "A half-dozen tenants, to say nothing of Mr. Searles himself, have looked it carefully over. All the walls are intact; there is absolutely no opening anywhere for surreptitious access."

"Possibly not. You certainly discourage me very much. I had hoped much from my theory. But we are not done with the matter. Mrs. Packard's mind must be cleared of its fancies, if it is in my power to do it. You will hear from me again, Mr. Robinson. Meanwhile, I may be sure of your good will?"

"Certainly, certainly, and of my cooperation also, if you want it."

"Thank you," said I, and left the office.

His last look was one of interest not untinged by compassion.

CHAPTER XI

BESS

On my way back I took the opposite side of the street from that I usually approached. When I reached the little shop I paused. First glancing at the various petty articles exposed in the window, I quietly stepped in. A contracted and very low room met my eyes, faintly lighted by a row of panes in the upper half of the door and not at all by the window, which was hung on the inside with a heavy curtain. Against two sides of this room were arranged shelves filled with boxes labeled in the usual way to indicate their contents. These did not strike me as being very varied or of a very high order. There was no counter in front, only some tables on which lay strewn fancy boxes of thread and other useless knick- knacks to which certain shop-keepers appear to cling though they can seldom find customers for them. A woman stood at one of these tables untangling a skein of red yarn. Behind her I saw another leaning in an abstracted way over a counter which ran from wall to wall across the extreme end of the shop. This I took to be Bess. She had made no move at my entrance and she made no move now. The woman with the skein appeared, on the contrary, as eager to see as the other seemed indifferent. I had to buy something and I did so in as matter-of-fact a way as possible, considering that my attention was more given to the woman in the rear than to the articles I was purchasing.

"You have a very convenient place here," I casually remarked, as I handed out my money. With this I turned squarely about and looked directly at her whom I believed to be Bess.

A voluble answer from the woman at my side, but not the wink of an eye from the one whose attention I had endeavored to attract.

"I live in the house opposite," I carelessly went on, taking in every detail of the strange being I was secretly addressing.

"Oh!" she exclaimed in startled tones, roused into speech at last. "You live opposite; in Mayor Packard's house?"

I approached her, smiling. She had dropped her hands from her chin and seemed very eager now, more eager than the other woman, to interest me in what she had about her and so hold me to the shop.

"Look at this," she cried, holding up an article of such cheap workmanship that I wondered so sensible an appearing woman would cumber her shelves with it. "I am glad you live over there," for I had nodded to her question. "I'm greatly interested in that house. I've worked there as cook and waitress several times."

I met her look; it was sharp and very intelligent.

"Then you know its reputation," I laughingly suggested.

She made a contemptuous gesture. The woman was really very good-looking, but baffling in her manner, as Mr. Robinson had said, and very hard to classify. "That isn't what interests me," she protested. "I've other reasons. You're not a relative of the family, are you?" she asked impetuously, leaning over the table to get a nearer view of my face.

"No, nor even a friend. I am in their employ just now as a companion to Mrs. Packard. Her health is not very good, and the mayor is away a great deal."

"I thought you didn't belong there. I know all who belong there. I've little else to do but stare across the street," she added apologetically and with a deep flush. "Business is very poor in this shop."

I was standing directly in front of her. Turning quickly about, I looked through the narrow panes of the door, and found that my eyes naturally rested on the stoop of the opposite house. Indeed, this stoop was about all that could be seen from the spot where this woman stood.

"Another eve bent in constant watchfulness upon us," I inwardly commented. "We are quite surrounded. The house should certainly hold treasure to warrant all this interest. But what could this one-time domestic know of the missing bonds?"

"An old-fashioned doorway," I remarked. "It is the only one of the kind on the whole street. It makes the house conspicuous, but in a way I like. I don't wonder you enjoy looking at it. To me such a house and such a doorway suggest mystery and a romantic past. If the place is not haunted—and only a fool believes in ghosts—something strange must have happened there or I should never have the nervous feeling I have in going about the halls and up and down the stairways. Did you never have that feeling?"

"Never. I'm not given to feelings. I live one day after another and just wait."

Not given to feelings! With such eyes in such a face! You should have looked down when you said that, Bess; I might have believed you then.

"Wait?" I softly repeated. "Wait for what? For fortune to enter your little shop-door?"

"No, for my husband to come back," was her unexpected answer, uttered grimly enough to have frightened that husband away again, had he been fortunate or unfortunate enough to hear her. "I'm a married woman, Miss, and shouldn't be working like this. And I won't be always; my man'll come back and make a lady of me again. It's that I'm waiting for."

Here a customer came in. Naturally I drew back, for our faces were nearly touching.

"Don't go," she pleaded, catching me by the sleeve and turning astonishingly pale for one ordinarily so ruddy. "I want to ask a favor of you. Come into my little room behind. You won't regret it." This last in an emphatic whisper.

Amazed at the turn which the conversation had taken and congratulating myself greatly upon my success in insuring her immediate confidence, I slipped through the opening she made for me between the tables serving for a counter and followed her into a room at the rear, which from its appearance answered the triple purpose of sleeping-room, parlor and kitchen.

"Pardon my impertinence," said she, as she carefully closed the door behind us. "It's not my habit to make friends with strangers, but I've taken a fancy to you and think you can be trusted. Will—" she hesitated, then burst out, "will you do something for me?"

"If I can," I smiled.

"How long do you expect to stay over there?"

"Oh, that I can't say."

"A month? a week?"

"Probably a week."

"Then you can do what I want. Miss—"

"Saunders," I put in.

"There is something in that house which belongs to me."

I started; this was hardly what I expected her to say.

"Something of great importance to me; something which I must have and have very soon. I don't want to go there for it myself. I hid it in a very safe place one day when my future looked doubtful, and I didn't know where I might be going or what might happen to me. Mrs. Packard would think it strange if she saw where, and might make it very uncomfortable for me. But you can get what I want without trouble if you are not afraid of going about the house at night. It's a little box with my name on it; and it is hidden—"

"Where?"

"Behind a brick I loosened in the cellar wall. I can describe the very place. Oh, you think I am asking too much of you—a stranger and a lady."

"No, I'm willing to do what I can for you. But I think you ought to tell me what's in the box, so that I shall know exactly what I am doing."

"I can't tell; I do not dare to tell till I have it again in my own hand. Then we will look it over together. Do you hesitate? You needn't; no inconvenience will follow to any one, if you are careful to rely on yourself and not let any other person see or handle this box."

"How large is it?" I asked, quite as breathless as herself, as I realized the possibilities underlying this remarkable request.

"It is so small that you can conceal it under an apron or in the pocket of your coat. In exchange for it, I will give you all I can afford—ten dollars."

"No more than that?" I asked, testing her.

"No more at first. Afterward—if it brings me what it ought to, I will give you whatever you think it is worth. Does that satisfy you? Are you willing to risk an encounter with the ghost, for just ten dollars and a promise?"

The smile with which she said this was indescribable. I think it gave me a more thrilling consciousness of human terror in face of the supernatural than anything which I had yet heard in this connection. Surely her motive for remaining in the haunted house had been extraordinarily strong.

"You are afraid," she declared. "You will shrink, when the time comes, from going into that cellar at night."

I shook my head; I had already regained both my will-power and the resolution to carry out this adventure to the end.

"I will go," said I.

"And get me my box?"

"Yes!"

"And bring it to me here as early the next day as you can leave Mrs. Packard?"

"Yes."

"Oh, you don't know what this means to me."

I had a suspicion, but held my peace and let her rhapsodize.

"No one in all my life has ever shown me so much kindness! Are you sure you won't be tempted to tell any one what you mean to do?"

"Quite sure."

"And will go down into the cellar and get this box for me, all by yourself?"

"Yes, if you demand it."

"I do; you will see why some day."

"Very well, you can trust me. Now tell me where I am to find the brick you designate."

"It's in the cellar wall, about half-way down on the right-hand side. You will see nothing but stone for a foot or two above the floor, but after that comes the brick wall. On one of these bricks you will detect a cross scratched. That's the one. It will look as well cemented as the rest, but if you throw water against it, you will find that in a little while you will be able to pry it out. Take something to do this with, a knife or a pair of scissors. When the brick falls out, feel behind with your hand and you will find the box."

"A questionable task. What if I should be seen at it?"

"The ghost will protect you!"

Again that smile of mingled sarcasm and innuendo. It was no common servant girl's smile, any more than her language was that of the ignorant domestic.

"I believe the ghost fails to walk since the present tenants came into the house," I remarked.

"But its reputation remains; you'll not be disturbed."

"Possibly not; a good reason why you might safely undertake the business yourself. I can find some way of letting you in."

"No, no. I shall never again cross that threshold!" Her whole attitude showed revolt and bitter determination.

"Yet you have never been frightened by anything there?"

"I know; but I have suffered; that is, for one who has no feelings. The box will have to remain in its place undisturbed if you won't get it for me."

"Positively?"

"Yes, Miss; nothing would induce me even to cross the street. But I want the box."

"You shall have it," said I.

CHAPTER XII

SEARCHINGS

I seemed bound to be the prey of a divided duty. As I crossed the street, I asked myself which of the two experiments I had in mind should occupy my attention first. Should I proceed at once with that close study and detailed examination of the house, which I contemplated in my eagerness to establish my theory of a secret passage between it and the one now inhabited by the Misses Quinlan, or should I wait to do this until I had recovered the box, which might hold still greater secrets?

I could not decide, so I resolved to be guided by circumstances. If Mrs. Packard were still out, I did not think I could sit down till I had a complete plan of the house as a start in the inquiry which interested me most.

Mrs. Packard was still out,—so much Nixon deigned to tell me in answer to my question. Whether the fact displeased him or not I could not say, but he was looking very sour and seemed to resent the trouble he had been to in opening the door for me. Should I notice this, even by an attempt to conciliate him? I decided not. A natural manner was best; he was too keen not to notice and give his own interpretation to uncalled for smiles or words which contrasted too strongly with his own marked reticence. I therefore said nothing as he pottered slowly back into his own quarters in the rear, but lingered about down-stairs till I was quite sure he was out of sight and hearing. Then I came back and took up my point of view on the spot where the big hall clock had stood in the days of Mr. Dennison. Later, I made a drawing of this floor as it must have looked at that time. You will find it on the opposite page.

[transcriber's note: The plan shows the house to have two rows of rooms with a hall between. In the front each room ends in a bow window. On the right the drawing-room has two doors opening into the hall, equally spaced near the front and rear of the room. Across the hall are two rooms of apparently equal size; a reception room in front and the library behind it, both rooms having windows facing on the alley. There is a stairway in the hall just behind the door to the reception room. The study is behind the drawing- room. Opposite this is a side hall and the dining-room. The library and dining-room both open off this hall with the dining room also having doors to the main hall and kitchen. The side hall ends with a stoop in the alley. A small room labeled kitchen, etc. lies behind the dining-room and the hall extends beyond the study beside the kitchen with the cellar stairs on the kitchen side. There is a small rectangle in the hall about two-thirds of the way down the side of the drawing-room which is labeled A.]

Near the place where I stood (marked A on the plan), had occurred most of the phenomena, which could be located at all. Here the spectral hand had been seen stopping the clock. Here the shape had passed encountered by Mr. Weston's cook, and just a few steps beyond where the library door opened under the stairs Mr. Searles had seen the flitting figure which had shut his mouth on the subject of his tenants' universal folly. From the front then toward the back these manifestations had invariably peeped to disappear—where? That was what I was to determine; what I am sure Mayor Packard would wish me to determine if he knew the whole situation as I knew it from his wife's story and the record I had just read at the agent's office.

Alas! there were many points of exit from this portion of the hall. The drawing-room opened near; so did Mayor Packard's study; then there was the kitchen with its various offices, ending as I knew in the cellar stairs. Nearer I could see the door leading into the dining-room and, opening closer yet, the short side hall running down to what had once been the shallow vestibule of a small side entrance, but which, as I had noted many times in passing to and from the dining-room, was now used as a recess or alcove to hold a cabinet of Indian curios. In which of these directions should I carry my inquiry? All looked equally unpromising, unless it was Mayor Packard's study, and that no one with the exception of Mr. Steele ever entered save by his invitation, not even his wife. I could not hope to cross that threshold, nor did I greatly desire to invade the kitchen, especially while Nixon was there. Should I have to wait till the mayor's return for the cooperation my task certainly demanded? It looked that way. But before yielding to the discouragement following this thought, I glanced about me again and suddenly remembered, first the creaking board, which had once answered to the so-called spirit's flight, and secondly the fact which common sense should have suggested before, that if my theory were true and the secret presence, whose coming and going I had been considering, had fled by some secret passage leading to the neighboring house, then by all laws of convenience and natural propriety that passage should open from the side facing the Quinlan domicile, and not from that holding Mayor Packard's study and the remote drawing-room.

This considerably narrowed my field of inquiry, and made me immediately anxious to find that creaking board which promised to narrow it further yet.

Where should I seek it? In these rear halls, of course, but I hated to be caught pacing them at this hour. Nixon's step had not roused it or I should have noticed it, for I was, in a way, listening for this very sound. It was not in the direct path then from the front door to the kitchen. Was it on one side or in the space about the dining-room door or where the transverse corridor met the main hall? All these floors were covered in the old- fashioned way with carpet, which would seem to show that no new boards had been laid and that the creaking one should still be here.

I ventured to go as far as the transverse hall,—I was at full liberty to enter the library. But no result followed this experiment; my footsteps had never fallen more noiselessly. Where could the board be? In aimless uncertainty I stepped into the corridor and instantly a creak woke under my foot. I had located the direction in which one of the so-called phantoms had fled. It was down this transverse hall.

Flushed with apparent success, I looked up at the walls on either side of me. They were gray with paint and presented one unbroken surface from base-board to ceiling, save where the two doorways opened, one into the library, the other into the dining-room. Had the flying presence escaped by either of these two rooms? I knew the dining-room well. I had had several opportunities for studying its details. I thought I knew the library; besides, Mr. Searles had been in the library when the shape advanced upon him from the hall,—a fact eliminating that room as a possible source of approach! What then was left? The recess which had once served as an old-time entrance. Ah, that gave promise of something. It projected directly toward where the adjacent walls had once held two doors, between which any sort of mischief might take place. Say that the Misses Quinlan had retained certain keys. What easier than for one of them to enter the outer door, strike a light, open the inner one and flash this light up through the house till steps or voices warned her of an aroused family, when she had only to reclose the inside door, put out the light and escape by the outer one.

But alas! at this point I remembered that this, as well as all other outside doors, had invariably been protected by bolt, and that these bolts had never been found disturbed. Veritably I was busying myself for nothing over this old vestibule. Yet before I left it I gave it another glance; satisfied myself that its

Anna Katherine Green

walls were solid; in fact, built of brick like the house. This on two sides; the door occupied the third and showed the same unbroken coat of thick, old paint, its surface barely hidden by the cabinet placed at right angles to it. Enough of it, however, remained exposed to view to give me an opportunity of admiring its sturdy panels and its old-fashioned lock. The door was further secured by heavy pivoted bars extending from jamb to jamb. An egg-and-dart molding extended all around the casing, where the inner door had once hung. All solid, all very old-fashioned, but totally unsuggestive of any reasonable solution of the mystery I had vaguely hoped it to explain. Was I mistaken in my theory, and must I look elsewhere for what I still honestly expected to find? Undoubtedly; and with this decision I turned to leave the recess, when a sensation, of too peculiar a nature for me readily to understand it, caused me to stop short, and look down at my feet in an inquiring way and afterward to lift the rug on which I had been standing and take a look at the floor underneath. It was covered with carpet, like the rest of the hall, but this did not disguise the fact that it sloped a trifle toward the outside wall. Had not the idea been preposterous, I should have said that the weight of the cabinet had been too much for it, causing it to sag quite perceptibly at the base-board. But this seemed too improbable to consider. Old as the house was, it was not old enough for its beams to have rolled. Yet the floor was certainly uneven, and, what was stranger yet, had, in sagging, failed to carry the base- board with it. This I could see by peering around the side of the cabinet. Was it an important enough fact to call for expla-nation? Possibly not; yet when I had taken a short leap up and come down on what was certainly an unstable floor, I decided that I should never be satisfied till I had seen that cabinet removed and the floor under it rigidly examined.

Yet when I came to take a look at this projection from the library window and saw that this floor, like that of the many entrances, was only the height of one step from the ground, I felt the folly into which my inquiring spirit had led me, and would have dismissed the whole subject from my mind if my eyes had not detected at that moment on one of the tables an unusually thin paper-knife. This gave me an idea. Carrying it back with me into the recess, I got down on my knees, and first taking the precaution to toss a little stick-pin of mine under the cabinet to be reached after in case I was detected there by Nixon, I insinuated the cutter between the base-board and the floor and found that I could not only push it in an inch or more before striking the brick, but run it quite freely around from one corner of the recess to the other. This was surely surprising. The exterior of this vestibule must be considerably larger than the interior would denote. What occupied the space between? I went upstairs full of thought. Sometime, and that before long, I would have that cabinet removed.

CHAPTER XIII

A DISCOVERY

Mrs. Packard came in very soon after this. She was accompanied by two friends and I could hear them talking and laughing in her room upstairs all the afternoon. It gave me leisure, but leisure was not what I stood in need of, just now. I desired much more an opportunity to pursue my inquiries, for I knew why she had brought these friends home with her and lent herself to a merriment that was not natural to her. She wished to forestall thought; to keep down dread; to fill the house so full of cheer that no whisper should reach her from that spirit-world she had come to fear. She had seen—or believed that she had seen—a specter, and she had certainly heard a laugh that had come from no explicable human source.

The brightness of the sunshiny day aided her unconsciously in this endeavor. But I foresaw the moment when this brightness would disappear and her friends say good-by. Then the shadows must fall again more heavily than ever, because of their transient lifting. I almost wished she had indeed gone with her husband, and found myself wondering why he had not asked her to do so when he found what it was that depressed her. Perhaps he had, and it was she who had held back. She may have made up her mind to conquer this weakness, and to conquer it where it had originated and necessarily held the strongest sway. At all events, he was gone and she was here, and I had done nothing as yet to relieve that insidious dread with which she must anticipate a night in this house without his presence.

I wondered if it would be any relief to her to have Mr. Steele remain upon the premises. I had heard him come in about three o'clock and go into the study, and when the time came for her friends to take their leave, and their voices in merry chatter came up to my ear from the open boudoir door, I stole down to ask her if I could suggest it to him. But I was too late. Just as I reached the head of the stairs on the second floor he came out of the study below and passed, hat in hand, toward the front door.

"What a handsome man!" came in an audible whisper from one of the ladies, who now stood in the lower hall.

"Who is he?" asked the other.

I thought he held the door open one minute longer than was necessary to catch her reply. It was a very cold and unenthusiastic one.

"That is Mr. Packard's secretary," said she. "He will join the mayor just as soon as he has finished certain preparations intrusted to him."

"Oh!" was their quiet rejoinder, but a note of disappointment rang in both voices as the door shut behind him.

"One does not often see a perfectly handsome man."

I stepped down to meet her when she in turn had shut the door upon them.

But I stopped half-way. She was standing with her head turned away from me and the knob still in her hand. I saw that she was thinking or was the prey of some rapidly growing resolve.

Suddenly she seized the key and turned it.

Anna Katherine Green

"The house is closed for the night," she announced as she looked up and met my astonished gaze. "No one goes out or comes in here again till morning. I have seen all the visitors I have strength for."

And though she did not know I saw it, she withdrew the key and slipped it into her pocket. "This is Nixon's night out," she murmured, as she led the way to the library. "Ellen will wait on us and we'll have the baby down and play games and be as merry as ever we can be,—to keep the ghosts away," she cried in fresh, defiant tones that had just the faintest suggestion of hysteria in them. "We shall succeed; I don't mean to think of it again. I'm right in that, am I not? You look as if you thought so. Ah, Mr. Packard was kind to secure me such a companion. I must prove my gratitude to him by keeping you close to me. It was a mistake to have those light-headed women visit me to-day. They tired more than they comforted me."

I smiled, and put the question which concerned me most nearly.

"Does Nixon stay late when he goes out?"

She threw herself into a chair and took up her embroidery.

"He will to-night," was her answer. "A little grandniece of his is coming on a late train from Pittsburgh. I don't think the train is due till midnight, and after that he's got to take her to his daughter's on Carey Street. It will be one o'clock at least before he can be back."

I hid my satisfaction. Fate was truly auspicious. I would make good use of his absence. There was nobody else in the house whose surveillance I feared.

"Pray send for the baby now," I exclaimed. "I am eager to begin our merry evening."

She smiled and rang the bell for Letty, the nurse.

Late that night I left my room and stole softly down-stairs. Mrs. Packard had ordered a bed made up for herself in the nursery and had retired early. So had Ellen and Letty. The house was therefore clear below stairs, and after I had passed the second story I felt myself removed from all human presence as though I were all alone in the house.

This was a relief to me, yet the experience was not a happy one. Ellen had asked permission to leave the light burning in the hall during the mayor's absence, so the way was plain enough before me; but no parlor floor looks inviting after twelve o'clock at night, and this one held a secret as yet unsolved, which did not add to its comfort or take the mysterious threat from the shadows lurking in corners and under stairways which I had to pass. As I hurried past the place where the clock had once stood, I thought of the nurses' story and of the many frightened hearts which had throbbed on the stairway I had just left and between the walls I was fast approaching; but I did not turn back. That would have been an acknowledgment of the truth of what I was at this very time exerting my full faculties to disprove.

I knew little about the rear of the house and nothing about the cellar. But when I had found my way into the kitchen and lit the candle I had brought from my room, I had no difficulty in deciding which of the many doors led below. There is something about a cellar door which is unmistakable, but it took me a minute to summon up courage to open it after I had laid my hand on its old-fashioned latch. Why do we so hate darkness and the chill of unknown regions, even when we know they are empty of all that can hurt or really frighten us? I was as safe there as in my bed up-stairs, yet I had to force myself to consider more than once the importance of my errand and the positive result it might have in allaying the disturbance in more than one mind, before I could lift that latch and set my foot on the short flight which led into the yawning blackness beneath me.

But once on my way I took courage. I pictured to myself the

collection of useful articles with which the spaces before me were naturally filled, and thought how harmless were the sources of the grotesque shadows which bowed to me from every side and even from the cement floor toward the one spot where the stones of the foundation showed themselves clear of all encumbering objects. As I saw how numerous these articles were, and how small a portion of the wall itself was really visible, I had my first practical fear, and a practical fear soon puts imaginary ones to flight. What if some huge box or case of bottles should have been piled up in front of the marked brick I was seeking? I am strong, but I could not move such an object alone, and this search was a solitary one; I had been forbidden to seek help.

The anxiety this possibility involved nerved me to instant action. I leaped forward to the one clear spot singled out for me by chance and began a hurried scrutiny of the short strip of wall which was all that was revealed to me on the right-hand side. Did it hold the marked brick? My little candle shook with eagerness and it was with difficulty I could see the face of the brick close enough to determine. But fortune favored, and presently my eye fell on one whose surface showed a ruder, scratched cross. It was in the lowest row and well within reach of my hand. If I could move it the box would soon be in my possession—and what might that box not contain!

Looking about, I found the furnace and soon the gas-jet which made attendance upon it possible. This lit, I could set my candle down, and yet see plainly enough to work. I had shears in my pocket. I have had a man's training in the handling of tools and felt quite confident that I could pry this brick out if it was as easily loosened as Bess had given me to understand. My first thrust at the dusty cement inclosing it encouraged me greatly. It was very friable and so shallow that my scissors'-point picked it at once. In five minutes' time the brick was clear, so that I easily lifted it out and set it on the floor. The small black hole which was left was large enough to admit my hand. I wasted no time thrusting it in, expecting to feel the box at once and draw it out. But it was farther back than I expected, and while I was feeling about something gave way and fell with a slight, rustling noise down out of my reach. Was it the box? No, for in another instant I had come in contact with its broken edges and had drawn it out; the falling object must have been some extra mortar, and it had gone where? I did not stop to consider then. The object in my hand was too alluring; the size, the shape too suggestive of a package of folded bonds for me to think of anything but the satisfaction of my curiosity and the consequent clearing of a very serious mystery.

Just at this moment, one of intense excitement, I heard, or thought I heard, a stealthy step behind me. Forcing myself to calmness, however, I turned and, holding the candle high convinced myself that I was alone in the cellar.

Carrying the box nearer the light, I pulled off its already loosened string and lifted the cover. In doing this I suffered from no qualms of conscience. My duty seemed very clear to me, and the end, a totally impersonal one, more than justified the means.

A folded paper met my eyes—one—not of the kind I expected; then some letters whose address I caught at a glance. "Elizabeth Brainard"—a discovery which might have stayed my hand at another time, but nothing could stay it now. I opened the paper and looked at it. Alas! it was only her marriage certificate; I had taken all this trouble and all this risk, only to rescue for her the proof of her union with one John Silverthorn Brainard. The same name was on her letters. Why had Bess so strongly insisted on a secret search, and why had she concealed her license in so strange a place?

Greatly sobered, I restored the paper to its place in the box, slipped on the string and prepared to leave the cellar with it. Then I remembered the brick on the floor and the open hole where it had been, and afterward the something which had fallen over within and what this space might mean in a seemingly solid wall.

Anna Katherine Green

More excited now even than I had been at any time before, I thrust my hand in again and tried to sound the depth of this unexpected far-reaching hole; but the size of my arm stood in the way of my experiment, and, drawing out my hand, I looked about for a stick and finding one, plunged that in. To my surprise and growing satisfaction it went in its full length—about three feet. There was a cavity on the other side of this wall of very sizable dimensions. Had I struck the suspected passage? I had great hope of it. Nothing else would account for so large a space on the other side of a wall which gave every indication of being one with the foundation. Catching up my stick I made a rude estimate of its location, after which I replaced the brick, put out the gas, and caught up Bess' box. Trembling, and more frightened now than at my descent at my own footfall and tremulous pursuing shadow, I went up-stairs.

As I passed the corridor leading to the converted vestibule which had so excited my interest in the afternoon, I paused and made a hurried calculation. If the stick had been three feet long, as I judged, and my stride was thirty inches, then the place of that hole in the wall below was directly in a line with where I now stood,—in other words, under the vestibule floor, as I had already, suspected.

How was I to verify this without disturbing Mrs. Packard? That was a question to sleep on. But it took me a long time to get to sleep.

CHAPTER XIV

I SEEK HELP

A bad night, a very bad night, but for all that I was down early the next morning. Bess must have her box and I a breath of fresh air before breakfast, to freshen me up a bit and clear my mind for the decisive act, since my broken rest had failed to refresh me.

As I reached the parlor floor Nixon came out of the reception-room.

"Oh, Miss!" he exclaimed, "going out?" surprised, doubtless, to see me in my hat and jacket.

"A few steps," I answered, and then stopped, not a little disturbed; for in moving to open the door he had discovered that the key was not in it and was showing his amazement somewhat conspicuously.

"Mrs. Packard took the key up to her room," I explained, thinking that some sort of explanation was in order. "She is nervous, you know, and probably felt safer with it there."

The slow shake of his head had a tinge of self-reproach in it.

"I was sorry to go out," he muttered. "I was very sorry to go out,"—but the look which he turned upon me the next minute was of a very different sort. "I don't see how you can go out yet," said he, "unless you go by the back way. That leads into Stanton Street; but perhaps you had just as lief go into Stanton Street."

There was impertinence in his voice as well as aggressiveness in his eye, but I smiled easily enough and was turning toward the back with every expectation of going by way of Stanton Street, when Letty came running down the stairs with the key in her hand. I don't think he was pleased, but he opened the door civilly enough and I gladly went out, taking with me, however, a remembrance of the furtive look with which he had noted the small package in my hand. I pass over the joy with which Bess received the box and its desired contents. I had lost all interest in the matter, which was so entirely personal to herself, and, declining the ten dollars which I knew she could ill afford, made my visit so short that I was able to take a brisk walk down the street and yet be back in time for breakfast.

This, like that of the preceding day, I took alone. Mrs. Packard was well but preferred to eat up-stairs. I did not fret at this; I was really glad, for now I could think and plan my action quite unembarrassed by her presence. The opening under the vestibule floor was to be sounded, and sounded this very morning, but on what pretext? I could not take Mrs. Packard into my counsel, for that would be to lessen the force of the discovery with which I yet hoped to dissipate at one blow the superstitious fears I saw it was otherwise impossible to combat. I might interest Ellen, and I was quite certain that I could interest the cook; but this meant Nixon, also, who was always around and whose animosity to myself was too mysteriously founded for me to trust him with any of my secrets or to afford him any inkling of my real reason for being in the house.

Yet help I must have and very efficient help, too. Should I telegraph to Mayor Packard for some sort of order which would lead to the tearing up of this end of the house? I could not do this without fuller explanations than I could give in a telegram. Besides, he was under sufficient pressure just now for me to spare him the consideration of so disturbing a matter, especially as he had left a substitute behind whose business it was, not only to relieve Mrs. Packard in regard to the libelous paragraph, but in all other directions to which his attention might be called. I would see Mr. Steele; he would surely be able to think up some scheme by which that aperture might be investigated without creating too much disturbance in the house.

An opportunity for doing this was not long in presenting itself. Mr. Steele came in about nine o'clock and passed at once into the study. The next moment I was knocking at his door, my heart in any mouth, but my determination strung up to the point of daring anything and everything for the end I had in view.

Fortunately he came to the door; I could never have entered without his encouragement. As I met his eye I was ashamed of the color my cheeks undoubtedly showed, but felt reconciled the next minute, for he was not quite disembarrassed himself, though he betrayed it by a little extra paleness rather than by a flush, such as had so disturbed myself. Both of us were quite natural in a moment, however, and answering his courteous gesture I stepped in and at once opened up my business.

"You must pardon me," said I, "for this infringement upon the usual rules of this office. I have something very serious to say about Mrs. Packard—oh, she's quite well; it has to do with a matter I shall presently explain—and I wish to make a request."

"Thank you for the honor," he said, drawing up a chair for me.

But I did not sit, neither did I speak for a moment. I was contemplating his features and thinking how faultless they were.

"I hardly know where to begin," I ventured at last. "I am burdened with a secret, and it may all appear puerile to you. I don't know whether to remind you first of Mayor Packard's intense desire to see his wife's former cheerfulness restored—a task in which I have been engaged to assist—or to plunge at once into my discoveries, which are a little peculiar and possibly important, in spite of my short acquaintance with the people under this roof and the nature of my position here."

"You excite me," were his few quick but sharply accentuated words. "What secret? What discoveries? I didn't know that the house held any that were worth the attention of sensible persons like ourselves."

I had not been looking at him directly, but I looked up at this and was astonished to find that his interest in what I had said was greater than appeared from his tone or even from his manner.

"You know the cause of Mrs. Packard's present uneasiness?" I asked.

"Mayor Packard told me—the paragraph which appeared in yesterday morning's paper. I have tried to find out its author, but I have failed so far."

"That is a trifle," I said. "The real cause—no, I prefer to stand," I put in, for he was again urging me by a gesture to seat myself.

"The real cause—" he repeated.

"—is one you will smile at, but which you must nevertheless respect. She thinks—she has confided to us, in fact—that she has seen, within these walls, what many others profess to have seen. You understand me, Mr. Steele?"

"I don't know that I do, Miss Saunders."

"I find it hard to speak it; you have heard, of course, the common gossip about this house."

"That it is haunted?" he smiled, somewhat disdainfully.

"Yes. Well, Mrs. Packard believes that she has seen what—what gives this name to the house."

"A ghost?"

"Yes, a ghost—in the library one night."

"Ah!"

The ejaculation was eloquent. I did not altogether understand it, but its chief expression seemed to be contempt. I began to fear he would not have sufficient sympathy with such an unreasoning state of mind to give me the attention and assistance I desired. He saw the effect it had upon me and hastened to say:

"The impression Mrs. Packard has made upon me was of a common-sense woman. I'm sorry to hear that she is the victim of an hallucination. What do you propose to do about it?—for I see that you have some project in mind."

Then I told him as much of my story as seemed necessary to obtain his advice and to secure his cooperation. I confided to him my theory of the unexplainable sights and sounds which had so unfortunately aroused Mrs. Packard's imagination, and what I had done so far to substantiate it. I did not mention the bonds, nor tell him of Bess and her box, but led him to think that my experiments in the cellar had been the result of my discoveries in the side entrance.

He listened gravely—I hardly feel justified in saying with a surprise that was complimentary. I am not sure that it was. Such men are difficult to understand. When I had finished, he remarked with a smile:

"So you conclude that the floor of this place is movable and that the antiquated ladies you mention have stretched their old limbs in a difficult climb, just for the game of frightening out tenants they did not desire for neighbors?"

"I know that it sounds ridiculous," I admitted, refraining still, in spite of the great temptation, from mentioning the treasure which it was the one wish of their lives to protect from the discovery of others. "If they were quite sane I should perhaps not have the courage to suggest this explanation of what has been heard and seen here. But they are not quite sane; a glance at their faces is enough to convince one of this, and from minds touched with insanity anything can be expected. Will you go with me to this side entrance and examine the floor for yourself? The condition of things under it I will ask you to take my word for; you will hardly wish to visit the cellar on an exploring expedition till you are reasonably assured of its necessity."

His eye, which had grown curiously cold and unresponsive through this, turned from me toward the desk before which he had been sitting. It was heaped high with a batch of unopened letters, and I could readily understand what was in his mind.

"You will be helping the mayor more by listening to me," I continued earnestly, "than by anything you can do here. Believe me, Mr. Steele, I am no foolish, unadvised girl. I know what I am talking about."

He suppressed an impatient sigh and endeavored to show a proper appreciation of my own estimate of myself and the value of my communication.

"I am at your service," said he.

I wished he had been a little more enthusiastic, but, careful not to show my disappointment, I added, as I led the way to the door:

"I wish we could think of some way of securing ourselves from interruption. Nixon does not like me, and will be sure to interest himself in our movements if he sees us go down that hall together."

"Is there any harm in that?"

"There might be. He is suspicious of me, which makes it impossible for one to count upon his conduct. If he saw us meddling with the cabinet, he would be very apt to rush with his complaints to Mrs. Packard, and I am not ready yet to take her into our confidence. I want first to be sure that my surmises are correct."

"You are quite right." If any sarcasm tinged this admission, he successfully hid it. "I think I can dispose of Nixon for a short time," he went on. "You are bent upon meddling with that vestibule floor?"

"Yes."

"Even if I should advise not?"

"Yes, Mr. Steele; even if you roused the household and called Mrs. Packard down to witness my folly. But I should prefer to make my experiments quickly and without any other witness than yourself. I am not without some pride to counterbalance my presumption."

We had come to a stand before the door as I said this. As I finished, he laid his hand on the knob, saying kindly:

"Your wishes shall be considered. Take a seat in the library, Miss Saunders, and in a few moments I will join you. I have a task for Nixon which will keep him employed for some time."

At this he opened the door and I glided out. Making my way to the library I hastened in and threw myself into one of its great chairs. In another minute I heard Mr. Steele summon Nixon, and in the short interview which followed between them heard enough to comprehend that he was loading the old butler's arms with a large mass of documents and papers for immediate consumption in the furnace. Nixon was not to leave till they were all safely consumed. The grumble which followed from the old fellow's lips was not the most cheerful sound in the world, but he went back with his pile. Presently I heard the furnace door rattle and caught the smell, which I was careful to explain to Ellen as she went by the library door on her way up-stairs, lest Mrs. Packard should be alarmed and come running down to see what was the matter.

The next moment Mr. Steele appeared in the doorway.

"Now what are we to do?" said he.

I led the way to what I have sometimes called "the recess" for lack of a better name.

"This is the place," I cried, adding a few explanations as I saw the curiosity with which he now surveyed its various features. "Don't you see now that cabinet leans to the left? I declare it leans more than it did yesterday; the floor certainly dips at that point."

He cast a glance where I pointed and instinctively put out his hand, but let it fall as I remarked:

"The cabinet is not so very heavy. If I take out a few of those big pieces of pottery, don't you think we could lift it away from this corner?"

"And what would you do then?"

"Tear up the carpet and see what is the matter with this part of the floor. Perhaps we shall find not only that, but something else of a still more interesting nature"

He was standing on the sill of what had been the inner doorway. As I said these words he fell back in careless grace against the panel and remained leaning there in an easy attitude, assumed possibly just to show me with what incredulity, and yet with what kindly forbearance he regarded my childish enthusiasm.

"I don't understand," said he. "What do you expect to find?"

"Some spring or button by which this floor is made to serve the purpose of a trap. I'm sure that there is an opening underneath—a large opening. Won't you help me—"

I forgot to finish. In my eagerness to impress him I had turned in his direction, and was staring straight at his easy figure and faintly smiling features, when the molding against which he leaned caught my eye. With a total absence of every other thought than the idea which had suddenly come to me, I sprang forward and pressed with my whole weight against one of the edges of the molding which had a darker hue about it than the rest. I felt it give, felt the floor start from under me at the same moment, and in another heard the clatter and felt the force of the toppling cabinet on my shoulder as it and I went shooting down into the hole I had been so anxious to penetrate, though not in just this startling fashion.

The cry, uttered by Mr. Steele as I disappeared from before his eyes, was my first conscious realization of what had happened after I had struck the ground below.

"Are you hurt?" he cried, with real commiseration, as he leaned over to look for me in the hollow at his feet. "Wait and I will drop down to you," he went on, swinging himself into a position to leap.

I was trembling with the shock and probably somewhat bruised, but not hurt enough to prevent myself from scrambling to my feet, as he slid down to my side and offered me his arm for support.

"What did you do?" he asked. "Was it you who made this trap give way? I see that it is a trap now,"—and he pointed to the square boarding hampered by its carpet which hung at one side.

"I pressed one of those round knobs in the molding," I explained, laughing to hide the tears of excitement in my eyes. "It had a loose look. I did it without thinking,—that is, without thinking enough of what I was doing to be sure that I was in a safe enough position for such an experiment. But I'm all right, and so is the cabinet. See!" I pointed to where it stood, still upright, its contents well shaken up but itself in tolerably good condition.

"You are fortunate," said he. "Shall I help you up out of this? Your curiosity must be amply satisfied."

"Not yet, not yet," I cried. "Oh! it is as I thought," I now exclaimed, peering around the corner of the cabinet into a place of total darkness. "The passage is here, running directly under the alley-way. Help me, help me, I must follow it to the end. I'm sure it communicates with the house next door."

He had to humor me. I already had one hand on the cabinet's edge, and should have pushed it aside by my own strength if he had not interfered. The space we were in was so small, some four feet square, I should judge, that the utmost we could do was to shove one corner of it slightly aside, so as to make a narrow passage into the space beyond. Through this I slipped and should have stepped recklessly on if he had not caught me back and suggested that he go first into what might have its own pitfalls and dangers.

I did not fear these, but was glad, nevertheless, to yield to his suggestion and allow him to pass me. As he did so, he took out a match from his pocket and in another moment had lit and held it out. A long, narrow vaulting met our eyes, very rude and propped up with beams in an irregular way. It was empty save for a wooden stool or some such object which stood near our feet. Though the small flame was insufficient to allow us to see very far, I was sure that I caught the outlines of a roughly made door at the extreme end and was making for this door, careless of his judgment and detaining hand, when a quick, strong light suddenly struck me in the face. In the square hollow made by the opening of this door, I saw the figure of Miss Charity with a lighted lantern in her hand. She was coming my way. the secret of the ghostly visitations which had deceived so many people was revealed.

Anna Katherine Green

CHAPTER XV

HARDLY A COINCIDENCE

The old lady's eyes met ours without purpose or intelligence. It was plain that she did not see us; also plain that she was held back in her advance by some doubt in her beclouded brain. We could see her hover, as it were, at her end of the dark passage, while I held my breath and Mr. Steele panted audibly. Then gradually she drew back and disappeared behind the door, which she forgot to shut, as we could tell from the gradually receding light and the faint fall of her footsteps after the last dim flicker had faded away.

When she was quite gone, Mr. Steele spoke:

"You must be satisfied now," he said. "Do you still wish to go on, or shall we return and explain this accident to the girls whose voices I certainly hear in the hall overhead?"

"We must go back," I reluctantly consented. A wild idea had crossed my brain of following out my first impulse and of charging Miss Charity in her own house with the visits which had from time to time depopulated this house.

"I shall leave you to make the necessary explanations," said he. "I am really rushed with business and should be down-town on the mayor's affairs at this very moment."

"I am quite ready," said I. Then as I squeezed my way through between the corner of the cabinet and the foundation wall, I could not help asking him how he thought it possible for these old ladies to mount to the halls above from the bottom of the four-foot hole in which we now stood.

"The same way in which I now propose that you should," he replied, lifting into view the object we had seen at one side of the passage, and which now showed itself to be a pair of folding steps. "Canny enough to discover or perhaps to open this passage, they were canny enough to provide themselves with means of getting out of it. Shall I help you?"

"In a minute," I said. "I am so curious. How do you suppose they worked this trap from here? They did not press the spring in the molding."

He pointed to one side of the opening, where part of the supporting mechanism was now visible.

"They worked that. It is all simple enough on this side of the trap; the puzzle is about the other. How did they manage to have all this mechanism put in without rousing any one's attention? And why so much trouble?"

"Some time I will tell you," I replied, putting my foot on the step. "O girls!" I exclaimed, as two screams rang out above and two agitated faces peered down upon us. "I've had an accident and a great adventure, but I've solved the mystery of the ghost. It was just one of the two poor old ladies next door. They used to come up through this trap. Where is Mrs. Packard?"

They were too speechless with wonder to answer me. I had to reach up my arms twice before either of them would lend me a helping hand. But when I was once up and Mr. Steele after me, the questions they asked came so thick and fast that I almost choked in my endeavor to answer them and to get away. Nixon appeared in the middle of it, and, congratulating myself that Mr. Steele had been able to slip away to the study while I was talking to the girls, I went over the whole story again for his benefit, after which I stopped abruptly and asked again where Mrs. Packard was.

Nixon, with a face as black as the passage from which I had just escaped, muttered some words about queer doings for respectable people, but said nothing about his mistress unless the few words he added to his final lament about the cabinet contained some allusion to her fondness for the articles it held. We could all see that they had suffered greatly from their fall. Annoyed at his manner, which was that of a man personally aggrieved, I turned to Ellen. "You have just been up-stairs," I said. "Is Mrs. Packard still in the nursery?"

"She was, but not more than five minutes ago she slipped down- stairs and went out. It was just before the noise you made falling down into this hole."

Out! I was sorry; I wanted to disburden myself at once.

"Well, leave everything as it is," I commanded, despite the rebellion in Nixon's eye. "I will wait in the reception-room till she returns and then tell her at once. She can blame nobody but me, if she is displeased at what she sees."

Nixon grumbled something and moved off. The girls, full of talk, ran up-stairs to have it out in the nursery with Letty, and I went toward the front. How long I should have to stay there before Mrs. Packard's return I did not know. She might stay away an hour and she might stay away all day. I could simply wait. But it was a happy waiting. I should see a renewal of joy in her and a bounding hope for the future when once I told any tale. It was enough to keep me quiet for the three long hours I sat there with my face to the window, watching for the first sight of her figure on the crossing leading into our street.

When it came, it was already lunch-time, but there was no evidence of hurry in her manner; there was, rather, an almost painful hesitation. As she drew nearer, she raised her eyes to the house- front and I saw with what dread she approached it, and what courage it took for her to enter it at all.

The sight of my face at the window altered her expression, however, and she came quite cheerfully up the steps. Careful to forestall Nixon in his duty, I opened the front door, and, drawing her into the room where I had been waiting, I blurted out my whole story before she could remove her hat.

"O Mrs. Packard," I cried, "I have such good news for you. The thing you feared hasn't any meaning. The house was never haunted; the shadows which have been seen here were the shadows of real beings. There is a secret entrance to this house, and through it the old ladies next door, have come from time to time in search of their missing bonds, or else to frighten off all other people from the chance of finding them. Shall I show you where the place is?"

Her face, when I began, had shown such changes I was startled; but by the time I had finished a sort of apathy had fallen across it and her voice sounded hollow as she cried: "What are you telling me? A secret entrance we knew nothing about and the Misses Quinlan using it to hunt about these halls at night! Romantic, to be sure. Yes, let me see the place. It is very interesting and very inconvenient. Will you tell Nixon, please, to have this passage closed?"

I felt a chill. If it was interest she felt it was a very forced one. She even paused to take off her hat. But when I had drawn her through the library into the side hall, and shown her the great gap where the cabinet had stood, I thought she brightened a little and showed some of the curiosity I expected. But it was very easily appeased, and before I could have made the thing clear to her she was back in the library, fingering her hat and listening, as it seemed to me, to everything but my voice.

I did not understand it.

Making one more effort I came up close to her and impetuously cried out:

"Don't you see what this does to the phantasm you professed to have seen yourself once in this very spot? It proves it a myth, a product of your own imagination, something which it must certainly be impossible for you ever to fear again. That is why I made the search which has ended in this discovery. I wanted to rid you of your forebodings. Do assure me that I have. It will be such a comfort to me—and how much more to the mayor!"

Her lack-luster eyes fell; her fingers closed on the hat whose feathers she had been trifling with, and, lifting it, she moved softly into the reception-room and from there into the hall and up the front stairs. I stood aghast; she had not even heard what I had been saying.

By the time I had recovered my equanimity enough to follow, she had disappeared into her own room. It could not have been in a very comfortable condition, for there were evidences about the hall that it was being thoroughly swept. As I endeavored to pass the door, I inadvertently struck the edge of a little taboret standing in my way. It toppled and a little book lying on it slid to the floor; as I stooped to pick it up my already greatly disconcerted mind was still further affected by the glimpse which was given me of its title. It was this

THE ECCENTRICITIES OF GHOSTS AND COINCIDENCES SUGGESTING SPIRITUAL INTERFERENCE

Struck forcibly by a coincidence suggesting something quite different from spiritual interference, I allowed the book to open in my hand, which it did at this evidently frequently conned passage:

A book was in my hand and a strong light was shining on it and on me from a lamp on a near-by table. The story was interesting and I was following the adventures it was relating, with eager interest, when suddenly the character of the light changed, a mist seemed to pass before my eyes and, on my looking up, I saw standing between me and the lamp the figure of a man, which vanished as I looked, leaving in my breast an unutterable dread and in my memory the glare of two unearthly eyes whose menace could mean but one thing—death.

The next day I received news of a fatal accident to my husband.

I closed the little volume with very strange thoughts. If Mayor Packard had believed himself to have received an explanation of his wife's strange condition in the confession she had made of having seen an apparition such as this in her library, or if I had believed myself to have touched the bottom of the mystery absorbing this unhappy household in my futile discoveries of the human and practical character of the visitants who had haunted this house, then Mayor Packard and I had made a grave mistake.

CHAPTER XVI

IN THE LIBRARY

I was still in Mrs. Packard's room, brooding over the enigma offered by the similarity between the account I had just read and the explanation she had given of the mysterious event which had thrown such a cloud over her life, when, moved by some unaccountable influence, I glanced up and saw Nixon standing in the open doorway, gazing at me with an uneasy curiosity I was sorry enough to have inspired.

"Mrs. Packard wants you," he declared with short ceremony. "She's in the library." And, turning on his heel, he took his deliberate way down-stairs.

I followed hard after him, and, being brisk in my movements, was at his back before he was half-way to the bottom. He seemed to resent this, for he turned a baleful look back at me and purposely delayed his steps without giving me the right of way.

"Is Mrs. Packard in a hurry?" I asked. "If so, you had better let me pass."

He gave no appearance of having heard me; his attention had been caught by something going on at the rear of the hall we were now approaching. Following his anxious glance, I saw the door of the mayor's study open and Mrs. Packard come out. As we reached the lower step, she passed us on her way to the library. Wondering what errand had taken her to the study, which she was supposed not to visit, I turned to join her and caught a glimpse of the old man's face. It was more puckered, scowling and malignant of aspect than usual. I was surprised that Mrs. Packard had not noticed it. Surely it was not the countenance of a mere disgruntled servant. Something not to be seen on the surface was disturbing this old man; and, moving in the shadows as I was, I questioned whether it would not conduce to some explanation between Mrs. Packard and myself if I addressed her on the subject of this old serving-man's peculiar ways.

But the opportunity for doing this did not come that morning. On entering the library I was met by Mrs. Packard with the remark:

"Have you any interest in politics? Do you know anything about the subject?"

"I have an interest in Mayor Packard's election," I smilingly assured her; "and I know that in this I represent a great number of people in this town if not in the state."

"You want to see him governor? You desired this before you came to this house? You believe him to be a good man—the right man for the place?"

"I certainly do, Mrs. Packard."

"And you represent a large class who feel the same?"

"I think so, Mrs. Packard."

"I am so glad!" Her tone was almost hysterical. "My heart is set on this election," she ardently explained. "It means so much this year. My husband is very ambitious. So am I—for him. I would give—" there she paused, caught back, it would seem, by some warning thought. I took advantage of her preoccupation to scrutinize her features more closely than I had dared to do while she was directly addressing me. I found them set in the stern mold of profound feeling—womanly feeling, no doubt, but one actuated by causes far greater than the subject, serious as it was, apparently called for. She would give—

What lay beyond that give?

I never knew, for she never finished her sentence.

Observing the breathless interest her manner evoked, or possibly realizing how nearly she had come to an unnecessary if not unwise self-betrayal, she suddenly smoothed her brow and, catching up a piece of embroidery from the table, sat down with it in her hand.

"A wife is naturally heart and soul with her husband," she observed, with an assumption of composure which restored some sort of naturalness to the conversation. "You are a thinking person, I see, and what is more, a conscientious one. There are many, many such in town; many amongst the men as well as amongst the women. Do you think I am in earnest about this—that Mr. Packard's chances could be affected by—by anything that might be said about me? You saw, or heard us say, at least, that my name had been mentioned in the morning paper in a way not altogether agreeable to us. It was false, of course, but—" She started, and her work fell from her hands. The door-bell had rung and we could hear Nixon in the hall hastening to answer it.

"Miss Saunders," she hurriedly interposed with a great effort to speak naturally, "I have told Nixon that I wish to see Mr. Steele if he comes in this morning. I wish to speak to him about the commission intrusted to him by my husband. I confess Mr. Steele has not inspired me with the confidence that Mr. Packard feels in him and I rather shrink from this interview. Will you be good enough—rather will you show me the great kindness of sitting on that low divan by the fireplace where you will not be visible—see, you may have my work to busy yourself with—and if—he may not, you know—if he should show the slightest disposition to transgress in any way, rise and show yourself?"

I was conscious of flushing slightly, but she was not looking my way, and the betrayal cost me only a passing uneasiness. She had, quite without realizing it, offered me the one opportunity I most desired. In my search for a new explanation of Mrs. Packard's rapidly changing moods, I had returned to my first suspicion—the attraction and possibly the passion of the handsome secretary for herself. I had very little reason for entertaining such a possibility. I had seen nothing on his part to justify it and but little on hers.

Yet in the absence of every other convincing cause of trouble I allowed myself to dwell on this one, and congratulated myself upon the chance she now offered me of seeing and hearing how he would comport himself when he thought that he was alone with her. Assured by the sounds in the hall that Mr. Steele was approaching, I signified my acquiescence with her wishes, and, taking the embroidery from her hand, sat down in the place she had pointed out.

I heard the deep breath she drew, forgot in an instant my purpose of questioning her concerning Nixon, and settled myself to listen, not only to such words as must inevitably pass between them, but to their tones, to the unconscious sigh, to whatever might betray his feeling toward her or hers toward him, convinced as I now was that feeling of some kind lay back of an interview which she feared to hold without the support of another's secret presence.

The calm even tones of the gentleman himself, modulated to an expression of utmost deference, were the first to break the silence.

"You wish to see me, Mrs. Packard?"

"Yes." The tremble in this ordinary monosyllable was slight but quite perceptible. "Mr. Packard has given you a task, concerning the necessity of which I should be glad to learn your opinion. Do you think it wise to—to probe into such matters? Not that I mean to deter you. You are under Mr. Packard's orders, but a word from so experienced a man would be welcome, if only to reconcile me to an effort which must lead to the indiscriminate use of my name in quarters where it hurts a woman to imagine it used at all."

This, with her eyes on his face, of this I felt sure. Her tone was much too level for her not to be looking directly at him. To any response he might give of the same nature I had no clue, but his tone when he answered was as cool and deferentially polite as was to be expected from a man chosen by Mayor Packard for his private secretary. "Mrs. Packard, your fears are very natural. A woman shrinks from such inquiries, even when sustained by the consciousness that nothing can rob her name of its deserved honor. But if we let one innuendo pass, how can we prevent a second? The man who did this thing should be punished. In this I agree with Mayor Packard."

She stirred impulsively. I could hear the rustle of her dress as she moved, probably to lessen the distance between them. "You are honest with me?" she urged. "You do agree with Mr. Packard in this?"

His answer was firm, straightforward, and, as far as I could judge, free from any objectionable feature. "I certainly do, Mrs. Packard. The hesitation I expressed when he first spoke was caused by the one consideration mentioned,—my fear lest something might go amiss in C—to-night if I busied myself otherwise than with the necessities of the speech with which he is about to open his campaign."

"I see. You are very desirous that Mr. Packard should win in this election?"

"I am his secretary, and was largely instrumental in securing his nomination for governor," was the simple reply. There was a pause—how filled, I would have given half my expected salary to know. Then I heard her ask him the very question she had asked me.

"Do you think that in the event of your not succeeding in forcing an apology from the man who inserted that objectionable paragraph against myself—that—that such hints of something being wrong with me will in any way affect Mr. Packard's chances—lose him votes, I mean? Will the husband suffer because of some imagined lack in his wife?"

"One can not say." Thus appealed to, the man seemed to weigh his words carefully, out of consideration for her, I thought. "No real admirer of the mayor's would go over to the enemy from any such cause as that. Only the doubtful—the half-hearted—those who are ready to grasp at any excuse for voting with the other party, would allow a consideration of the mayor's domestic relations to interfere with their confidence in him as a public officer."

"But these—" How I wish I could have seen her face! "These half-hearted voters, their easily stifled convictions are what make majorities," she stammered. Mr. Steele may have bowed; he probably did, for she went on confidently and with a certain authority not observable in the tone of her previous remarks. "You are right. The paragraph reflecting on me must be traced to its source. The lie must be met and grappled with. I was not well last week and showed it, but I am perfectly well to-day and am resolved to show that, too. No skeleton hangs in the Packard closet. I am a happy wife and a happy mother. Let them come here and see. This morning I shall issue invitations for a dinner to be given the first night you can assure me Mr. Packard will be at home. Do you know of any such night?"

"On Friday week he has no speech to make." Mrs. Packard seemed to consider. Finally she said: "When you see him, tell him to leave that evening free. And, Mr. Steele, if you will be so good, give me the names of some of those halfhearted ones—critical people who have to see in order to believe. I shall have them at my table —I shall let them see that the shadow which enveloped me was ephemeral; that a woman can rise above all weakness in the support of a husband she loves and honors as I do Mr. Packard."

She must have looked majestic. Her voice thrilling with anticipated triumph rang through the room, awaking echoes which surely must have touched the heart of this man if, as I had sometimes thought, he cherished an unwelcome admiration for her.

But when he answered, there was no hint in his finely modulated tones of any chord having been touched in his breast, save the legitimate one of respectful appreciation of a woman who fulfilled the expectation of one alive to what is admirable in her sex.

"Your idea is a happy one," said he. "I can give you three names now. Those of Judge Whittaker, Mr. Dumont, the lawyer, and the two Mowries, father and son."

"Thank you. I am indebted to you, Mr. Steele, for the patience with which you have met and answered my doubts."

He made some reply, added something about not seeing her again till he returned with the mayor, then I heard the door open and quietly shut. The interview was over, without my having felt called upon to show myself. An interval of silence, and then I heard her voice. She had thrown herself down at the piano and was singing gaily, ecstatically.

Approaching her in undisguised wonder at this new mood, I stood at her back and listened. I do not suppose she had what is called a great voice, but the feeling back of it at this moment of reaction gave it a great quality. The piece—some operatic aria—was sung in a way to thrill the soul. Opening with a burst, it ended with low notes of an intense sweetness like sobs, not of grief, but happiness. In their midst and while the tones sank deepest, a child's voice rose in the hall and we heard, uttered at the very door:

"Mama busy; mama sing."

With a cry she sprang from the piano and, bounding to the door, flung it open and caught her child in her arms.

"Darling! darling! my darling!" she exclaimed in a burst of mother-rapture, crushing the child to her breast and kissing it repeatedly.

Then she began to dance, holding the baby in her arms and humming a waltz. As I stood on one side in my own mood of excited sympathy, I caught fleeting glimpses of their two faces, as she went whirling about. Hers was beautiful in her new relief—if it was a relief—the child's dimpled with delight at the rapid movement—a lovely picture. Letty, who stood waiting in the doorway, showed a countenance full of surprise. Mrs. Packard was the first to feel tired. Stopping her dance, she peered round at the baby's face and laughed.

"Was that good?" she asked. "Are you glad to have mama merry again? I am going to be merry all the time now. With such a dear, dear dearie of a baby, how can I help it?" And whirling about in my direction, she held up the child for inspection, crying: "Isn't she a darling! Do you wonder at my happiness?"

Indeed I did not; the sweet baby-face full of glee was irresistible; so was the pat-pat of the two dimpled hands on her mother's shoulders. With a longing all women can understand, I held out my own arms.

"I wonder if she will come to me?" said I.

But though I got a smile, the little hands closed still more tightly round the mother's neck.

"Mama dear!" she cried, "mama dear!" and the tender

emphasis on the endearing word completed the charm. Tears sprang to Mrs. Packard's eyes, and it was with difficulty that she passed the clinging child over to the nurse waiting to take her out.

"That was the happiest moment of my life!" fell unconsciously from Mrs. Packard's lips as the two disappeared; but presently, meeting my eyes, she blushed and made haste to remark:

"I certainly did Mr. Steele an arrant injustice. He was very respectful; I wonder how I ever got the idea he could be anything else."

Anxious myself about this very fact, I attempted to reply, but she gave me no opportunity.

"And now for those dinner invitations!" she gaily suggested. "While I feel like it I must busy myself in making out my list. It will give me something new to think about."

CHAPTER XVIII

THE TWO WEIRD SISTERS

Ellen seemed to understand my anxiety about Mrs. Packard and to sympathize with it. That afternoon as I passed her in the hall she whispered softly:

"I have just been unpacking that bag and putting everything back into place. She told me she had packed it in readiness to go with Mr. Packard if he desired it at the last minute."

I doubted this final statement, but the fact that the bag had been unpacked gave me great relief. I began to look forward with much pleasure to a night of unbroken rest.

Alas! rest was not for me yet. Relieved as to Mrs. Packard, I found my mind immediately reverting to the topic which had before engrossed it, though always before in her connection. The mystery of the so-called ghosts had been explained, but not the loss of the bonds, which had driven my poor neighbors mad. This was still a fruitful subject of thought, though I knew that such well-balanced and practical minds as Mayor Packard's or Mr. Steele's would have but little sympathy with the theory ever recurring to me. Could this money be still in the house?—the possibility of such a fact worked and worked upon my imagination till I grew as restless as I had been over the mystery of the ghosts and presently quite as ready for action.

Anna Katherine Green

Possibly the hurried glimpse I had got of Miss Thankful's countenance a little while before, in the momentary visit she paid to the attic window at which I had been accustomed to see either her or her sister constantly sit, inspired me with my present interest in this old and wearing trouble of theirs and the condition into which it had thrown their minds. I thought of their nights of broken rest while they were ransacking the rooms below and testing over and over the same boards, the same panels for the secret hiding-place of their lost treasure, of their foolish attempts to scare away all other intruders, and the racking of nerve and muscle which must have attended efforts so out of keeping with their age and infirmities.

It would be natural to regard the whole matter as an hallucination on their part, to disbelieve in the existence of the bonds, and to regard Miss Thankful's whole story to Mrs. Packard as the play of a diseased imagination.

But I could not, would not, carry my own doubts to this extent. The bonds had been in existence; Miss Thankful had seen them; and the one question calling for answer now was, whether they had been long ago found and carried off, or whether they were still within the reach of the fortunate hand capable of discovering their hiding-place.

The nurse who, according to Miss Thankful, had wakened such dread in the dying man's breast as to drive him to the attempt which had ended in this complete loss of the whole treasure, appeared to me the chief factor in the first theory. If any one had ever found these bonds, it was she; how, it was not for me to say, in my present ignorant state of the events following the reclosing of the house after this old man's death and burial. But the supposition of an utter failure on the part of this woman and of every other subsequent resident of the house to discover this mysterious hiding-place, wakened in me no real instinct of search. I felt absolutely and at once that any such effort in my present blind state of mind would be totally unavailing. The secret trap and the passage it led to, with all the opportunities they offered for the concealment of a few folded documents, did not, strange as it may appear at first blush, suggest the spot where these papers might be lying hid. The manipulation of the concealed mechanism and the difficulties attending a descent there, even on the part of a well man, struck me as precluding all idea of any such solution to this mystery. Strong as dying men sometimes are in the last flickering up of life in the speedily dissolving frame, the lowering of this trap, and, above all, the drawing of it back into place, which I instinctively felt would be the hardest act of the two, would be beyond the utmost fire or force conceivable in a dying man. No, even if he, as a member of the family, knew of this subterranean retreat, he could not have made use of it. I did not even accept the possibility sufficiently to approach the place again with this new inquiry in mind. Yet what a delight lay in the thought of a possible finding of this old treasure, and the new life which would follow its restoration to the hands which had once touched it only to lose it on the instant.

The charm of this idea was still upon me when I woke the next morning. At breakfast I thought of the bonds, and in the hour which followed, the work I was doing for Mrs. Packard in the library was rendered difficult by the constant recurrence of the one question into my mind: "What would a man in such a position do with the money he was anxious to protect from the woman he saw coming and secure to his sister who had just stepped next door?" When a moment came at last in which I could really indulge in these intruding thoughts, I leaned back in my chair and tried to reconstruct the room according to Mrs. Packard's description of it at that time. I even pulled my chair over to that portion of the room where his bed had stood, and, choosing the spot where his head would naturally lie, threw back my own on the reclining chair I had chosen, and allowed my gaze to wander over the walls before me in a vague hope of reproducing, in my mind, the ideas which must have passed through his before he rose and thrust those papers into their place of concealment. Alas! those walls were barren of all suggestion, and my eyes went wandering through the window before me in a vague appeal, when a sudden remembrance of his last moments struck me sharply and I bounded up with a new thought, a new idea, which sent me in haste to my room and brought me down again in hat and jacket. Mrs. Packard had once said that the ladies next door were pleased to have callers, and advised me to visit them. I would test her judgment in the matter. Early though it was, I would present myself at the neighboring door and see what my reception would be. The discovery I had made in my unfortunate accident in the old entry way should be my excuse. Apologies were in order from us to them; I would make these apologies.

I was prepared to confront poverty in this bare and comfortless-looking abode of decayed gentility. But I did not expect quite so many evidences of it as met my eyes as the door swung slowly open some time after my persistent knock, and I beheld Miss Charity's meager figure outlined against walls and a flight of uncarpeted stairs such as I had never seen before out of a tenement house. I may have dropped my eyes, but I recovered myself immediately. Marking the slow awakening of pleasure in the wan old face as she recognized me, I uttered some apology for my early call and then waited to see if she would welcome me in.

She not only did so, but did it with such a sudden breaking up of her rigidity into the pliancy of a naturally hospitable nature, that my heart was touched, and I followed her into the great bare apartment, which must have once answered the purposes of a drawing- room, with very different feelings from those with which I had been accustomed to look upon her face in the old attic window.

"I should like to see your sister, too," I said, as she hastily, but with a certain sort of ceremony, too, pushed forward one of the ancient chairs which stood at long intervals about the room. "I have not been your neighbor very long, but I should like to pay my respects to both of you."

I had purposely spoken with the formal precision she had been accustomed to in her earlier days, and I could see how perceptibly her self-respect returned at this echo of the past, giving her a sudden dignity which made me forget for the moment her neglected appearance.

"I will summon my sister," she returned, disappearing quietly from the room.

I waited fifteen minutes, then Miss Thankful entered, dressed in her very best, followed by my first acquaintance in her same gown, but with a little cap on her head. The cap, despite its faded ribbons carefully pressed out but with too cold an iron, gave her an old-time fashionable air which for the moment created the impression that she might have been a beauty and a belle in her early days, which I afterward discovered to be true.

It was Miss Thankful, however, who had the personal presence, and it was she who now expressed their sense of the honor, pushing forward another chair than that from which I had risen, with the remark:

"Take this, I pray. Many an honored guest has occupied this seat. Let us see you in it."

I could detect no difference between the one she offered and the one in which I had just sat, but I at once stepped forward and took the chair she proffered. She bowed and Miss Charity bowed, and then they seated themselves side by side on the hair-cloth sofa, which was the only other article of furniture in the room.

"We are—we are preparing to move," stammered Miss Charity, a faint flush tingeing her faded cheeks, as she caught the involuntary glance I had cast about me.

Miss Thankful bridled and gave her sister a look of open rebuke. She had, as one could instantly see from her strong features and purposeful ways, been a woman of decided parts and of strict, upright character. Weakened as she was, the shadow of an untruth disturbed her. Her pride ran in a different groove from that of her once over-complimented, over-fostered sister. She was going to add a protest in words to that expressed by her gesture, but I hastily prevented this by coming at once to the point of my errand.

"My excuse for this early call," I said, this time addressing Miss Thankful, "lies in an adventure which occurred to me yesterday in the adjoining house." It was painful to see how they both started, and how they instinctively caught each at the other's hand as they sat side by side on the sofa, as if only thus they could bear the shock of what might be coming next. I had to nerve myself to proceed. "You know, or rather I gather from your kind greetings that you know that I am at present staying with Mrs. Packard. She is very kind and we spend many pleasant hours together; but of course some of the time I have to be alone, and then I try to amuse myself by looking about at the various interesting things which are scattered through the house."

A gasp from Miss Charity, a look still more expressive from Miss Thankful. I hastened to cut their suspense short.

"You know the little cabinet they have placed in the old entrance pointing this way? Well, I was looking at that when the whim seized me—I hardly know how—to press one of the knobs in the molding which runs about the doorway, when instantly everything gave way under me and I fell into a deep hole which had been scooped out of the alley-way—nobody knows for what."

A cry and they were on their feet, still holding hands and endeavoring to show nothing but concern for my disaster.

"Oh, I wasn't hurt," I smiled. "I was frightened, of course, but not so much as to lose my curiosity. When I got to my feet again, I looked about in this surprising hole—"

"It was our uncle's way of reaching his winecellar," Miss

Thankful explained with great dignity as she and her sister sank back into their seats. "He had some remarkable old wine, and, as he was covetous of it, he conceived this way of securing it from everybody's knowledge but his own. It was a strange way, but he was a little touched," she added, laying a slow impressive finger on her forehead, "just a little touched here."

The short, significant glance she cast at Charity as she said this, and the little smile she gave were to give me to understand that this weakness had descended in the family. I felt my heart contract; my self-imposed task was a harder one than I had anticipated, but I could not shirk it now. "Did this wine-cellar you mention run all the way to this house?" I lightly inquired. "I stumbled on a passage leading here, which I thought you ought to know is now open to any one in Mayor Packard's house. Of course, it will be closed soon," I hastened to add as Miss Charity hurriedly rose at her sister's quick look and anxiously left the room. "Mrs. Packard will see to that."

"Yes, yes, I have no doubt; she's a very good woman, a very fair woman, don't you think so, Miss—"

"My name is Saunders."

"A very good name. I knew a fine family of that name when I was younger. There was one of them—his name was Robert—" Here she rambled on for several minutes as if this topic and no other filled her whole mind; then, as if suddenly brought back to what started it, she uttered in sudden anxiety, "You think well of Mrs. Packard? You have confidence in her?"

I allowed myself to speak with all the enthusiasm she so greedily desired.

"Indeed I have," I cried. "I think she can be absolutely depended on to do the right thing every time. You are fortunate in having such good neighbors at the time of this mishap."

At this minute Miss Charity reentered. Her panting condition, as well as the unsettled position of the cap on her head, told very plainly where she had been. Reseating herself, she looked at Miss Thankful and Miss Thankful looked at her, but no word passed. They evidently understood each other.

"I'm obliged to Mrs. Packard," now fell from Miss Thankful's lips, "and to you, too, young lady, for acquainting us with this accident. The passage we extended ourselves after taking up our abode in this house. We—we did not see why we should not profit by our ancestor's old and undiscovered wine-cellar to secure certain things which were valuable to us."

Her hesitation in uttering this final sentence—a sentence all the more marked because naturally, she was a very straight-forward person—awoke my doubt and caused me to ask myself what she meant by this word "secure." Did she mean, as circumstances went to show and as I had hitherto believed, that they had opened up this passage for the purpose of a private search in their old home for the lost valuables they believed to be concealed there? Or had they, under some temporary suggestion of their disorganized brains, themselves hidden away among the rafters of this unexplored spot the treasure they believed lost and now constantly bewailed?

The doubt thus temporarily raised in my mind made me very uneasy for a moment, but I soon dismissed it and dropping this subject for the nonce, began to speak of the houses as they now looked and of the changes which had evidently been made in them since they had left the one and entered the other.

"I understand," I ventured at last, "that in those days this house also had a door opening on the alley-way. Where did it lead—do you mind my asking?—into a room or into a hallway? I am so interested in old houses."

They did not resent this overt act of curiosity; I had expected Miss Thankful to, but she didn't. Some recollection connected with the name of Saunders had softened her heart toward me and made her regard with indulgence an interest which she might otherwise have looked upon as intrusive.

"We long ago boarded up that door," she answered. "It was of very little use to us from our old library."

"It looked into one of the rooms then?" I persisted, but with a wary gentleness which I felt could not offend.

"No; there is no room there, only a passageway. But it has closets in it, and we did not like to be seen going to them any time of day. The door had glass panes in it, you know, just like a window. It made the relations so intimate with people only a few feet away."

"Naturally," I cried, "I don't wonder you wanted to shut them off if you could." Then with a sudden access of interest which I vainly tried to hide, I thought of the closets and said with a smile, "The closets were for china, I suppose; old families have so much china."

Miss Charity nodded, complacency in every feature; but Miss Thankful thought it more decorous to seem to be indifferent in this matter.

"Yes, china; old pieces, not very valuable. We gave what we had of worth to our sister when she married. We keep other things there, too, but they are not important. We seldom go to those closets now, so we don't mind the darkness."

"I—I dote on old china," I exclaimed, carefully restraining myself from appearing unduly curious. "Won't you let me look at it? I know that it is more valuable than you think. It will make me happy for the whole day, if you will let me see these old pieces. They may not look beautiful to you, you are so accustomed to them; but to me every one must have a history, or a history my imagination will supply."

Miss Charity looked gently but perceptibly frightened. She

shook her head, saying in her weak, fond tones:

"They are too dusty; we are not such housekeepers as we used to be; I am ashamed—"

But Miss Thankful's peremptory tones cut her short.

"Miss Saunders will excuse a little dust. We are so occupied," she explained, with her eye fixed upon me in almost a challenging way, "that we can afford little time for unnecessary housework. If she wants to see these old relics of a former day, let her. You, Charity, lead the way."

I was trembling with gratitude and the hopes I had suppressed, but I managed to follow the apologetic figure of the humiliated old lady with a very good grace. As we quitted the room we were in, through a door at the end leading into the dark passageway, I thought of the day when, according to Mrs. Packard's story, Miss Thankful had come running across the alley and through this very place to astound her sister and nephew in the drawing-room with the news of the large legacy destined so soon to be theirs. That was two years ago, and to-day—I proceeded no further with what was in my mind, for my interest was centered in the closet whose door Miss Charity had just flung open.

"You see," murmured that lady, "that we haven't anything of extraordinary interest to show you. Do you want me to hand some of them down? I don't believe that it will pay you."

I cast a look at the shelves and felt a real disappointment. Not that the china was of too ordinary a nature to attract, but that the pieces I saw, and indeed the full contents of the shelves, failed to include what I was vaguely in search of and had almost brought my mind into condition to expect.

"Haven't you another closet here?" I faltered. "These pieces are pretty, but I am sure you have some that are larger and with the pattern more dispersed—a platter or a vegetable dish."

"No, no," murmured Miss Charity, drawing back as she let the door slip from her hand. "Really, Thankful,"—this to her sister who was pulling open another door,—"the look of those shelves is positively disreputable—all the old things we have had in the house for years. Don't—"

"Oh, do let me see that old tureen up on the top shelf," I put in. "I like that."

Miss Thankful's long arm went up, and, despite Miss Charity's complaint that it was too badly cracked to handle, it was soon down and placed in my hands. I muttered my thanks, gave utterance to sundry outbursts of enthusiasm, then with a sudden stopping of my heart-beats, I lifted the cover and—

"Let me set it down," I gasped, hurriedly replacing the cover. I was really afraid I should drop it. Miss Thankful took it from me and rested it on the edge of the lower shelf.

"Why, how you tremble, child!" she cried. "Do you like old Colonial blue ware as well as that? If you do, you shall have this piece. Charity, bring a duster, or, better, a damp cloth. You shall have it, yes, you shall have it."

"Wait!" I could hardly speak. "Don't get a cloth yet. Come with me back into the parlor, and bring the tureen. I want to see it in full light."

They looked amazed, but they followed me as I made a dash for the drawing-room, Miss Thankful with the tureen in her hands. I was quite Mistress of myself before I faced them again, and, sitting down, took the tureen on my lap, greatly to Miss Charity's concern as to the injury it might do my frock.

"There is something I must tell you about myself before I can accept your gift," I said.

"What can you have to tell us about yourself that could make us hesitate to bestow upon you such an insignificant piece of old cracked china?" Miss Thankful asked as I sat looking up at them with moist eyes and wildly beating heart.

"Only this," I answered. "I know what perhaps you had rather have had me ignorant of. Mrs. Packard told me about the bonds you lost, and how you thought them still in the house where your brother died, though no one has ever been able to find them there. Oh, sit down," I entreated, as they both turned very pale and looked at each other in affright. "I don't wonder that you have felt their loss keenly; I don't wonder that you have done your utmost to recover them, but what I do wonder at is that you were so sure they were concealed in the room where he lay that you never thought of looking elsewhere. Do you remember, Miss Quinlan, where his eyes were fixed at the moment of death?"

"On the window directly facing his bed."

"Gazing at what?"

"Sky—no, the walls of our house."

"Be more definite; at the old side door through which he could see the closet shelves where this old tureen stood. During the time you had been gone, he had realized his sinking condition, and, afraid of the nurse he saw advancing down the street, summoned all his strength and rushed with his treasure across the alley-way and put it in the first hiding-place his poor old eyes fell on. He may have been going to give it to you; but you had company, you remember, in here, and he may have heard voices. Anyhow, we know that he put it in the tureen because—" here I lifted the lid—"because—" I was almost as excited and trembling and beside myself as they were— "because it is here now."

They looked, then gazed in each other's face and bowed their heads. Silence alone could express the emotion of that moment. Then with a burst of inarticulate cries, Miss Charity rose and solemnly began dancing up and down the great room.

Her sister looked on with grave disapproval till the actual nature of the find made its way into her bewildered mind, then she reached over and plunged her hand into the tureen and drew out the five bonds which she clutched first to her breast and then began proudly to unfold.

"Fifty thousand dollars!" she exclaimed. "We are rich women from to-day," and as she said it I saw the shrewdness creep beck into her eyes and the long powerful features take on the expressive character which they had so pitifully lacked up to the moment. I realized that I had been the witness of a miracle. The reason, shattered, or, let us say, disturbed by one shock, had been restored by another. The real Miss Thankful stood before me. Meanwhile the weaker sister, dancing still, was uttering jubilant murmurs to which her feet kept time with almost startling precision. But as the other let the words I have recorded here leave her lips, she came to a sudden standstill and approaching her lips to Miss Thankful's ear said joyfully:

"We must tell—oh," she hastily interpolated as she caught her sister's eyes and followed the direction of her pointing finger, "we have not thanked our little friend, our good little friend who has done us such an inestimable service." I felt her quivering arms fall round my neck, as Miss Thankful removed the tureen and in words both reasonable and kind expressed the unbounded gratitude which she herself felt.

"How came you to think? How came you to care enough to think?" fell from her lips as she kissed me on the forehead. "You are a jewel, little Miss Saunders, and some day—"

But I need not relate all that she said or all the extravagant things Miss Charity did, or even my own delight, so much greater even than any I had anticipated, when I first saw this possible ending of my suddenly inspired idea. However, Miss Thankful's words as we parted at the door struck me as strange, showing that it would be a little while yet before the full balance of her mind was restored.

"Tell everybody," she cried; "tell Mrs. Packard and all who live in the house; but keep it secret from the woman who keeps that little shop. We are afraid of her; she haunts this neighborhood to get at these very bonds. She was the nurse who cared for my brother, and it was to escape her greed that he hid this money. If she knew that we had found these our lives wouldn't be safe. Wait till we have them in the bank."

"Assuredly. I shall tell no one."

"But you must tell those at home," she smiled; and the beaming light in her kindled eye followed me the few steps I had to take, and even into the door.

So Bess had been the old man's nurse'!

CHAPTER XVIII

THE MORNING NEWS

That evening I was made a heroine of by Mrs. Packard and all the other members of the household. Even Nixon thawed and showed me his genial side. I had to repeat my story above stairs—and below, and relate just what the old ladies had done and said, and how they bore their joy, and whatever I thought they would do with their money now they had it. When I at last reached my room, my first act was to pull aside my shade and take a peep at the old attic window. Miss Charity's face was there, but so smiling and gay I hardly knew it. She kissed her hand to me as I nodded my head, and then turned away with her light as if to show me she had only been waiting to give me this joyous good night.

This was a much better picture to sleep on than the former one had been.

Next day I settled back into my old groove. Mrs. Packard busied herself with her embroidery and I read to her or played on the piano. Happier days seemed approaching, nay, had come. We enjoyed two days of it, then trouble settled down on us once more.

It began on Friday afternoon. Mrs. Packard and I had been out making some arrangements for the projected dinner-party and I had stopped for a minute in the library before going up-stairs.

Anna Katherine Green

A pile of mail lay on the table. Running this over with a rapid hand, she singled out several letters which she began to open. Their contents seemed far from satisfactory. Exclamation after exclamation left her lips, her agitation increasing with each one she read, and her haste, too, till finally it seemed sufficient for her just to glance at the unfolded sheet before letting it drop. When the last one had left her hand, she turned and, encountering my anxious look, bitterly remarked:

"We need not have made those arrangements this morning. Seven regrets in this mail and two in the early one. Nine regrets in all! and I sent out only ten invitations. What is the meaning of it? I begin to feel myself ostracized."

I did not understand it any more than she did.

"Invite others," I suggested, and was sorry for my presumption the next minute.

Her poor lip trembled.

"I do not dare," she whispered. "Oh, what will Mr. Packard say! Some one or something is working against us. We have enemies—enemies, and Mr. Packard will never get his election."

Her trouble was natural and so was her expression of it. Feeling for her, and all the more that the cause of this concerted action against her was as much a mystery to me as it was to herself, I made some attempt to comfort her, which was futile enough, God knows. She heard my voice, no doubt, but she gave no evidence of noting what I said. When I had finished—that is, when she no longer heard me speaking—she let her head droop and presently I heard her murmur:

"It seems to me that if for any reason he fails to get his election I shall wish to die."

She was in this state of dejection, with the echo of this sad sentence in both our ears, when a light tap at the door was followed by the entrance of Letty, the nurse-maid. She wore an unusual look of embarrassment and held something crushed in her hand. Mrs. Packard advanced hurriedly to meet her.

"What is it?" she interrogated sharply, like one expectant of evil tidings.

"Nothing! that is, not much," stammered the frightened girl, attempting to thrust her hand behind her back.

But Mrs. Packard was too quick for her.

"You have something there! What is it? Let me see."

The girl's hand moved forward reluctantly. "A paper which I found pinned to the baby's coat when I took her out of the carriage," she faltered. "I—I don't know what it means."

Mrs. Packard's eyes opened wide with horror. She seized the paper and staggered with it to one of the windows. While she looked at it, I cast a glance at Letty. She was crying, from what looked like pure fear; but it was the fear of ignorance rather than duplicity; she appeared as much mystified as ourselves.

Meanwhile I felt, rather than saw, the old shadow settling fast upon the head of her who an hour before had been so bright. She had chosen a place where her form could not fail of being more or less concealed by the curtain, and though I heard the paper rattle I could not see it or the hand which held it. But the time she spent over it seemed interminable before I heard her utter a sharp cry and saw the curtains shake as she clutched them.

It seemed the proper moment to proffer help, but before either Letty or I could start forward, her command rang out in smothered but peremptory tones:

"Keep back! I want no one here!" and we stopped, each

looking at the other in very natural consternation. And when, after another seemingly interminable interval, she finally stepped forth, I noted a haggard change in her face, and that her coat had been torn open and even the front of her dress wrenched apart as if she felt herself suffocating, or as if—but this alternative only suggested itself to me later and I shall refrain from mentioning it now.

Crossing the floor with a stumbling step, with the paper which had roused all this indignation still in her hand, she paused before the now seriously alarmed Letty, and demanded in great excitement:

"Who pinned that paper on my child? You know; you saw it done. Was it a man or—"

"Oh no, ma'am, no, ma'am," protested the girl. "No man came near her. It was a woman—a nice-looking woman."

"A woman!"

Mrs. Packard's tone was incredulous. But the girl insisted.

"Yes, ma'am; there was no man there at all. I was on one of the park benches resting, with the baby in my arms, and this woman passed by and saw us. She smiled at the baby's ways, and then stopped and took to talking about her,—how pretty she was and how little afraid of strangers. I saw no harm in the woman, ma'am, and let her sit down on the same bench with me for a few minutes. She must have pinned the paper on the baby's coat then, for it was the only time anybody was near enough to do it."

Mrs. Packard, with an irrepressible gesture of anger or dismay, turned and walked back to the window. The movement was a natural one. Certainly she was excusable for wishing to hide from the girl the full extent of the agitation into which this misadventure had thrown her.

"You may go." The words came after a moment of silent suspense. "Give the baby her supper—I know that you will never let any one else come so near her again."

Letty probably did not catch the secret anguish hidden in her tone, but I did, and after the nurse-maid was gone, I waited anxiously for what Mrs. Packard would say.

It came from the window and conveyed nothing. Would I do so and so? I forget what her requests were, only that they necessitated my leaving the room. There seemed no alternative but to obey, yet I felt loath to leave her and was hesitating near the doorway when a new interruption occurred. Nixon brought in a telegram, and, as Mrs. Packard advanced to take it, she threw on the table the slip of paper which she had been poring over behind the curtains.

As I stepped back at Nixon's entrance I was near the table and the single glance I gave this paper as it fell showed me that it was covered with the same Hebrew-like characters of which I already possessed more than one example. The surprise was acute, but the opportunity which came with it was one I could not let slip. Meeting her eye as the door closed on Nixon, I pointed at the scrawl she had thrown down, and wonderingly asked her if that was what Letty had found pinned to the baby's coat.

With a surprised start, she paused in her act of opening the telegram and made a motion as if to repossess herself of this, but seeming to think better of it she confined herself to giving me a sharp look.

"Yes," was her curt assent.

I summoned up all my courage, possibly all my powers of acting."

"Why, what is there in unreadable characters like these to alarm you?"

She forgot her telegram, she forgot everything but that here was a question she must answer in a way to disarm all suspicion.

"The fact," she accentuated gravely, "that they are unreadable. What menace may they not contain? I am afraid of them, as I am of all obscure and mystifying things."

In a flash, at the utterance of these words, I saw, my way to the fulfillment of the wish which had actuated me from the instant my eyes had fallen on this paper.

"Do you think it a cipher?" I asked.

"A cipher?"

"I have always been good at puzzles. I wish you would let me see what I can make out of these rows of broken squares and topsy-turvy angles. Perhaps I can prove to you that they contain nothing to alarm you."

The gleam of something almost ferocious sprang into this gentle woman's eyes. Her lips moved and I expected an angry denial, but fear kept her back. She did not dare to appear to understand this paper any better than I did. Besides, she was doubtless conscious that its secret was not one to yield to any mere puzzle-reader. She could safely trust it to my curiosity. All this I detected in her changing expression, before she made the slightest gesture which allowed me to secure what I felt to be the most valuable acquisition in the present exigency.

Then she turned to her telegram. It was from her husband, and I was not prepared for the cry of dismay which left her lips as she read it, nor for the increased excitement into which she was thrown by its few and seemingly simple words.

With apparent forgetfulness of what had just occurred—a forgetfulness which insensibly carried her back to the moment when she had given me some order which involved my departure from the room—she impetuously called out over her shoulder which she had turned on opening her telegram:

"Miss Saunders! Miss Saunders! are you there? Bring me the morning papers; bring me the morning papers!"

Instantly I remembered that we had not read the papers. Contrary to our usual habit we had gone about a pressing piece of work without a glance at any of the three dailies laid to hand in their usual place on the library table. "They are here on the table," I replied, wondering as much at the hectic flush which now enlivened her features as at the extreme paleness that had marked them the moment before.

"Search them! There is something new in them about me. There must be. Read Mr. Packard's message."

I took it from her hand; only eight words in all.

Here they are—the marks of separation being mine:

I am coming—libel I know—where is S.

Henry.

"Search the columns," she repeated, as I laid the telegram down. "Search! Search!"

I hastily obeyed. But it took me some time to find the paragraph I sought. The certainty that others in the house had read these papers, if we had not, disturbed me. I recalled certain glances which I had seen pass between the servants behind Mrs. Packard's back,—glances which I had barely noted at the time, but which returned to my mind now with forceful meaning; and if these busy girls had read, all the town had read—what? Suddenly I found it. She saw my eyes stop in their hurried scanning and my fingers clutch the sheet more firmly, and, drawing up behind me, she attempted to follow with her eyes the words I reluctantly read out. Here they are, just as they left my trembling lips that day—words that only the most rabid of opponents could have instigated:

Apropos of the late disgraceful discoveries, by which a woman of apparent means and unsullied honor has been precipitated from her proud preeminence as a leader of fashion, how many women, known and admired to-day, could stand the test of such an inquiry as she was subjected to? We know one at least, high in position and aiming at a higher, who, if the merciful veil were withdrawn which protects the secrets of the heart, would show such a dark spot in her life, that even the aegis of the greatest power in the state would be powerless to shield her from the indignation of those who now speak loudest in her praise.

"A lie!" burst in vehement protest from Mrs. Packard, as I finished. "A lie like the rest! But oh, the shame of it! a shame that will kill me." Then suddenly and with a kind of cold horror: "It is this which has destroyed my social prestige in town. I understand those nine declinations now. Henry! my poor Henry!"

There was little comfort to offer, but I tried to divert her mind to the practical aspect of the case by saying:

"What can Mr. Steele be doing? He does not seem to be very successful in his attempts to carry out the mayor's orders. See! your husband asks where he is. He can mean no other by the words 'Where is S—?' He knew that your mind would supply the name."

"Yes."

Her eyes had become fixed; her whole face betrayed a settled despair. Quickly, violently, she rang the bell.

Nixon appeared.

She advanced hurriedly to meet him.

"Nixon, you have Mr. Steele's address?"

"Yes, Mrs. Packard."

"Then go to it at once. Find Mr. Steele if you can, but if that is not possible, learn where he has gone and come right back and tell me. Mr. Packard telegraphs to know where he is. He has not joined the mayor in C—."

"Yes, Mrs. Packard; the house is not far. I shall be back in fifteen minutes."

The words were respectful, but the sly glint in his blinking eyes as he hastened out fixed my thoughts again on this man and the uncommon attitude he maintained toward the mistress whose behests he nevertheless flew to obey.

CHAPTER XIX

THE CRY FROM THE STAIRS

I was alone in the library when Nixon returned. He must have seen Mrs. Packard go up before he left, for he passed by without stopping, and the next moment I heard his foot on the stairs.

Some impulse made me step into the hall and cast a glance at his ascending figure. I could see only his back, but there was something which I did not like in the curve of that back and the slide of his hand as it moved along the stair-rail.

His was not an open nature at the best. I almost forgot the importance of his errand in watching the man himself. Had he not been a servant—but he was, and an old and foolishly fussy one. I would not imagine follies, only I wished I could follow him into Mrs. Packard's presence.

His stay, however, was too short for much to have been gained thereby. Almost immediately he reappeared, shaking his head and looking very much disturbed, and I was watching his pottering descent when he was startled, and I was startled, by two cries which rang out simultaneously from above, one of pain and distress from the room he had just left, and one expressive of the utmost glee from the lips of the baby whom the nursemaid was bringing down from the upper hall.

Appalled by the anguish expressed in the mother's cry, I was bounding up-stairs when my course was stopped by one of the most poignant sights it has ever been my lot to witness. Mrs. Packard had heard her child's laugh, and flying from her room had met the little one on the threshold of her door and now, crying and sobbing, was kneeling with the child in her arms in the open space at the top of the stairs. Her paroxysm of grief, wild and unconstrained as it was, gave less hint of madness than of intolerable suffering.

Wondering at an abandonment which bespoke a grief too great for all further concealment, I glanced again at Nixon. He had paused in the middle of the staircase and was looking back in a dubious way denoting hesitation. But as the full force of the tragic scene above made itself felt in his slow mind, he showed a disposition to escape and tremblingly continued his descent. He was nearly upon me when he caught my eye. A glare awoke in his, and seeing his right arm rise threateningly, I thought he would certainly strike me. But he slid by without doing so.

What did it mean? Oh, what did it all mean?

Anna Katherine Green

CHAPTER XX

EXPLANATION

Determined to know the cause of Mrs. Packard's anguish, if not of Nixon's unprovoked anger against myself, I caught him back as he was passing me and peremptorily demanded:

"What message did you carry to Mrs. Packard to throw her into such a state as this? Answer! I am in this house to protect her against all such disturbances. What did you tell her?"

"Nothing."

Sullenness itself in the tone.

"Nothing? and you were sent on an errand? Didn't you fulfil it?"

"Yes."

"And didn't tell her what you learned?"

"No."

"Why?"

"She didn't give me the chance."

"Oh!"

"I know it sounds queer, Miss, but it's true. She didn't give me a chance to talk."

He muttered the final sentence. Indeed, all that we had said until now had been in a subdued tone, but now my voice unconsciously rose.

"You found Mr. Steele?"

"No, Miss, he was not at home."

"But they told you where to look for him?"

"No. His landlady thinks he is dead. He has queer spells, and some one had sent her word about a man, handsome like him, who was found dead at Hudson Three Corners last night. Mr. Steele told her he was going over to Hudson Three Corners. She has sent to see if the dead man is he."

"The dead man!"

Who spoke? Not Mrs. Packard! Surely that voice was another's. Yet we both looked up to see:

The sight which met our eyes was astonishing, appalling. She had let her baby slip to the floor and had advanced to the stairs, where she stood, clutching at the rail, looking down upon us, with a joy in her face matching the unholy elation we could still hear ringing in that word "dead."

Such a look might have leaped to life in the eyes of the Medusa when she turned her beauty upon her foredoomed victims.

"Dead!" came again in ringing repetition from Mrs. Packard's lips, every fiber in her tense form quivering and the gleam of hope shining brighter and brighter in her countenance. "No, not dead!" Then while Nixon trembled and succumbed inwardly to this spectacle of a gentle-hearted woman transformed by some secret and overwhelming emotion into an image of vindictive delight, her hands left the stair-rail and flew straight up over her head in the transcendent gesture which only the greatest crises in life call forth, and she exclaimed with awe-inspiring emphasis: "God could not have been so merciful!"

It is not often, perhaps it is only once in a lifetime, that it is given us to look straight into the innermost recesses of the human soul. Never before had such an opportunity come to me, and possibly never would it come again, yet my first conscious impulse was one of fright at the appalling self-revelation she had made, not only in my hearing, but in that of nearly her whole household. I could see, over her shoulders, Letty's eyes staring wide in ingenuous dismay, while from the hall below rose the sound of hurrying feet as the girls came running in from the kitchen. Something must be done, and immediately, to recall her to herself, and, if possible, to reinstate her in the eyes of her servants.

Bounding upward to where she still stood forgetful and self-absorbed, I laid my hands softly but firmly on hers, which had fallen back upon the rail, and quietly said:

"You have some very strong reason, I see, for looking upon Mr. Steele as your husband's enemy rather than friend."

The appeal was timely. With a start she woke to the realization of her position and of the suggestive words she had just uttered, and with a glance behind her at Letty and another at Nixon and the maids, who by this time had pushed their way to the foot of the stairs, she gathered herself up with a determination born of the necessity of the moment and emphatically replied:

"No; I do not know Mr. Steele well enough for that. My emotion at the unexpected tidings of his possible death springs from another cause." Here the help, the explanation for which she had been searching, came. "Girls," she went on, addressing them with an emphasis which drew all eyes, "I am ashamed to tell you what has so deeply disturbed me these last few days. I should blame any one of you for being affected as I was. The great love I bear my husband and child is my excuse—a poor one, I know, but one you will understand. A week ago something happened to me in the library which frightened me very much. I saw—or thought I saw—what some would call an apparition, but what you would call a ghost. Don't shriek!" (The two girls behind me had begun to scream and make as if to run away.) "It was all imagination, of course—there can not really be any such thing. Ghosts in these days? Pshaw! But I was very, nervous that night and could not help feeling that the mere fact of my thinking of anything so dreadful meant misfortune to some one in this house. Wait!" Her voice was imperious; and the shivering, terrified girls, superstitious to the backbone, stopped in spite of themselves. "You must hear it all, and you, too, Miss Saunders, who have only heard half. I was badly frightened then, especially as the ghost, spirit-man, or whatever it was, wore a look, in the one short moment I stood face to face with it, full of threat and warning. Next day Mr. Packard introduced his new secretary. Girls, he had the face of the Something I had seen, without the threatening look, which had so alarmed me."

"Bad 'cess to him!" rang in vigorous denunciation from the cook. "Why didn't ye send him 'mejitly about his business? It's trouble he'll bring to us all and no mistake!"

"That was what I feared," assented her now thoroughly composed mistress. "So when Nixon said just now that Mr. Steele was dead, had fallen in a fit at Hudson Three Corners or something like that—I felt such wicked relief at finding that my experience had not meant danger to ourselves, but to him—wicked, because it was so selfish—that I forgot myself and cried out in the way you all heard. Blame me if you will, but don't frighten yourselves by talking about it. If Mr. Steele is indeed dead, we have enough to trouble us without that."

And with a last glance at me, which ended in a wavering half-deprecatory smile, she stepped back and passed into her own room.

The mood in which I proceeded to my own quarters was as thoughtful as any I had ever experienced.

CHAPTER XXI

THE CIPHER

Hitherto I had mainly admired Mrs. Packard's person and the extreme charm of manner which never deserted her, no matter how she felt. Now I found myself compelled to admire the force and quality of her mind, her readiness to meet emergencies and the tact with which she had availed herself of the superstition latent in the Irish temperament. For I had no more faith in the explanation she had seen fit to give these ignorant girls than I had in the apparition itself. Emotion such as she had shown called for a more matter-of-fact basis than the one she had ascribed to it. No unreal and purely superstitious reason would account for the extreme joy and self-abandonment with which she had hailed the possibility of Mr. Steele's death. The "no" she had given me when I asked if she considered this man her husband's enemy had been a lying no. To her, for some cause as yet unexplained, the secretary was a dangerous ally to the man she loved; an ally so near and so dangerous that the mere rumor of his death was capable of lifting her from the depths of despondency into a state of abnormal exhilaration and hope. Now why? What reason had she for this belief, and how was it in my power to solve the mystery which I felt to be at the bottom of all the rest?

But one means suggested itself. I was now assured that Mrs. Packard would never take me into her actual confidence, any more than she had taken her husband. What I learned must be in spite of her precautions. The cipher of which I had several

Anna Katherine Green

specimens might, if properly read, give me the clue I sought. I had a free hour before me. Why not employ it in an endeavor to pick out the meaning of those odd Hebraic characters? I had in a way received her sanction to do so—if I could; and if I should succeed, what shadows might it not clear from the path of the good man whose interests it was my chief duty to consult?

Ciphers have always possessed a fascination for me. This one, from the variety of its symbols, offered a study of unusual interest. Collecting the stray specimens which I had picked up, I sat down in my cozy little room and laid them all out before me, with the following result:

[transcriber's note: the symbols cannot be converted to ASCII so I have shown them as follows:]

[] is a Square

[-] is sides and bottom of a square,

C is top, bottom and left side of a square,

L is left side and bottom of a square,,

V is two lines forming a V shape

. appearing before a symbol should be inside the symbol

) appearing before a symbol means the mirror image of that symbol

^ appearing before a symbol means the inverted symbol

? is a curve inside the symbol

all other preceding symbols are my best approximation for shapes shown inside that symbol.

; is used to separate each symbol

---

1. []; V; []; .>; V; [-]; <;

2. []; V; []; .>; V; [-]; <; L;).L; <;)7; .7;

3. []; V; []; .>; V; [-]; <;).L; .C;[]; .L; >; ,C; []; .<; ^[-]; ^[-]; .<;

4. []; V; []; .>; V; [-]; <; <; L; >; ^V; L; V; [];)L; ^V; [-]; []; V;).C; ^[-]; >;)C;),C; V; <; C; ^V; ^[-]; .>; [-]; <;

5. *>; []; V; []; *V; []; ~7;)C; .>; ^[o];)L; ^V; []; Lo; ^V;)C;)7*; V;)C?; L;)L; 7; .>; .^[-];)L; >; <; :[-], [-]; Lo; .<; ?[-];)7; [-];)C; []; .C; [-]; *7; L; .7; ^V;)o7; *>; C; ^V; .C; .<; [-]; []; 7; .C;)L; :7; [-];)*L; C; ^V; .L; .>; ^[%]; C; 7; *L; 7;):L;)7; ^.V; []; [-]; .L;[-]

No. 1: My copy of the characters, as I remember seeing them on the envelope which Mrs. Packard had offered to Mr. Steele and afterward thrown into the fire.

Nos. 2, 3 and 4: The discarded scraps I had taken from the waste-basket in her room.

No. 5: The lengthy communication in another hand, which Mrs. Packard had found pinned on the baby's cloak, and at my intercession had handed over to me.

A goodly array, if the latter was a specimen of the same cipher as the first, a fact which its general appearance seemed to establish, notwithstanding the few added complexities observable in it, and one which a remembrance of her extreme agitation on opening it would have settled in my mind, even if these complexities had been greater and the differences even more pronounced than they were. Lines entirely unsuggestive of meaning to her might have aroused her wonder and possibly her anger, but not her fear; and the emotion which I chiefly observed in her at that moment had been fear.

So! out of these one hundred and fifty characters, many of them mere repetitions, it remained for me to discover a key whereby their meaning might be rendered intelligible.

To begin, then, what peculiarities were first observable in them?

Several.

First: The symbols followed one after the other without breaks, whether the communication was limited to one word or to many.

Second: Nos. 2, 3 and 4 started with the identical characters which made up No. 1.

Third: While certain lines in Nos. 2, 3 and 4 were heavier than others, no such distinction was observable in the characters forming No. 1.

Fourth: This distinction was even more marked in the longer specimen written by another hand, viz.: No. 5.

Fifth: This distinction, which we will call shading, occurred intermittently, sometimes in two consecutive characters, but never in three.

Sixth: This shading was to be seen now on one limb of the character it apparently emphasized and now on another.

Seventh: In the three specimens of the seven similar characters commencing Nos. 2, 3 and 4, the exact part shaded was not always the same as for instance, it was the left arm of the second character in No. 2 which showed the heavy line, while the shading was on the right-hand arm of the corresponding character in No. 3.

Eighth: These variations of emphasis in No. 4 coincided sometimes with those seen in No. 2 and again with those in No. 3.

Ninth: Each one of these specimens, saving the first, ended in a shaded character.

Tenth: While some of the characters were squares or parts of a square, others were in the shape of a Y turned now this way and now that.

Eleventh: These characters were varied by the introduction of dots, and, in some cases, by the insertion of minute sketches of animals, birds, arrows, signs of the zodiac, etc., with here and there one of a humorous, possibly sarcastic, nature.

Twelfth: Dots and dots only were to be found in the specimen emanating from Mrs. Packard's hand; birds, arrows, skipping boys and hanging men, etc., being confined to No. 5, the product of another brain and hand, at present unknown.

Now what conclusions could I draw from these? I shall give them to you as they came to me that night. Others with wits superior to my own may draw additional and more suggestive ones:

First: Division into words was not considered necessary or was made in some other way than by breaks.

Second: The fact of the shading being omitted from No. 1 meant nothing—that specimen being my own memory of lines, the shading or non-shading of which would hardly have attracted my attention.

Third: The similarity observable in the seven opening characters of the first four specimens being taken as a proof of their standing for the same word or phrase, it was safe to consider this word or phrase as a complete one to which she had tried to fit others, and always to her dissatisfaction, till she had finally rejected all but the simple one with which she had started.

Fourth: No. 1, short as it was, was, therefore, a communication in itself.

Fifth: The shading of a character was in some way essential to its proper understanding, but not the exact place where that shading fell.

Sixth: The dots were necessarily modifications, but not their shape or nature.

Seventh: This shading might indicate the end of a word.

Eighth: If so, the shading of two contiguous characters would show the first one to be a word of one letter. There are but two words in the English language of one letter—a and i—and in the specimens before me but one character, that of [], which shows shading, next to another shaded character.

Ninth: [] was therefore a or i

A decided start.

All this, of course, was simply preliminary.

The real task still lay before me. It was to solve the meaning of those first seven characters, which, if my theory were correct, was a communication in itself, and one of such importance that, once mastered, it would give the key to the whole situation.

[]; V; []; .>; V; [-]; <;

or with the shading (same in bold - transcriber)

[]; V; []; .>; V; [-]; <;

You have all read The Gold Bug, and know something of the method by which a solution is obtained by that simplest of all ciphers, where a fixed character takes the place of each letter in the alphabet.

Let us see if it applies to this one.

There are twenty-six letters in the English alphabet. Are there twenty-six or nearly twenty-six different characters, in the one hundred and one I find inscribed on the various slips spread out before me?

No, there are but fourteen. A check to begin with.

But wait; the dots make a difference. Let us increase the list by assuming that angles or squares thus marked are different letters from those of the same shape in which no dots or sketches occur, and we bring the list up to twenty. That is better.

The dotted or otherwise marked squares or angles are separate characters.

Now, which one of these appears most frequently? The square, which we have already decided must be either a or i. In the one short word or phrase we are at present considering, it occurs twice. Now supposing that this square stands for a, which according to Poe's theory it should, a coming before s in the frequency in which it occurs in ordinary English sentences, how would the phrase look (still according to Poe) with dashes taking the place of the remaining unknown letters?

Thus

A-a—if the whole is a single word.

A-a- — if the whole is a phrase. That it was a phrase I was convinced, possibly because one clings to so neat a theory as the one which makes the shading, so marked a feature in all the specimens before us, the sign of division into words. Let us take these seven characters as a phrase then and not as a word. What follows?

The dashes following the two a's stand for letters, each of which should make a word when joined to a. What are these letters? Run over the alphabet and see. The only letters making sense when joined with a are h, m, n, s, t or x. Discarding the first and the last, we have these four words, am, an, as, at. Is it possible to start any intelligible phrase with any two of these arranged in any conceivable way? No. Then [] can not stand for a. Let us see if it does for i. The words of two letters headed by i we find to be if, in, is and it. A more promising collection than the first. One could easily start a phrase with any of these, even with any two of them such as If it, Is in, Is it, It is. [] is then the symbol of i, and some one of the above named combinations forms the beginning of the short phrase ending with a word of three letters symbolized by V [-] .<

What word?

If my reasoning is correct up to this point, it should not be hard to determine.

First, one of these three symbols, the V, is a repetition of one of those we have already shown to be s, t, f, or n. Of the remaining two, [-] <, one must be a vowel, that is, it must be either u, e, o, u, or y; i being already determined upon. Now how many [-]'s and <'s do we find in the collection before us? Ten or more of the first, and six, or about six, of the latter. Recalling the table made out by Poe—a table I once learned as a necessary part of my schooling as a cipher interpreter—I ran over it thus: e is the one letter most in use in English. Afterward the succession runs thus a, o, i d, h, n, r, etc. There being then ten [-]'s to six <'s [-] must be a vowel, and in all probability the vowel e, as no other character in the whole collection, save the plentiful squares, is repeated so often.

I am a patient woman usually, but I was nervous that night,

and, perhaps, too deeply interested in the outcome to do myself justice. I could think of no word with a for one of its three letters which would make sense when added on to It is, Is it, I f it, Is in.

Conscious of no mistake, yet always alive to the possibility of one, I dropped the isolated scrap I was working upon and took up the longer and fuller ones, and with them a fresh line of reasoning. If my argument so far had been trustworthy, I should find, in these other specimens, a double [-][-] standing for the double e so frequently found in English. Did I find such? No. Another shock to my theory.

Should I, then, give it up? Not while another means of verification remained. The word the should occur more than once in a collection of words as long as the one before me. If U is really e, I should find it at the end of the supposed thes. Do I so find it? There are several words scattered through the whole, of only three letters. Are any of them terminated by U? Not one. My theory is false, then, and I must begin all over.

Discarding every previous conclusion save this, that the shading of a line designated the termination of a word, I hunted first for the thes. Making a list of the words containing only three letters, I was confronted by the following:

V [-] <

)L)C C

< L >

^V L V

< C ^V

.> .[-]))L

.V).C L.

.< .[-])7

^V C 7

)L .L >

No two alike. Astonishing! Thirty-two words of English and only one *the* in the whole? Could it be that the cipher was in a foreign language? The preponderance of *i*'s so out of proportion to the other vowels had already given me this fear, but the lack of *thes* seemed positively to indicate it. Yet I must dig deeper before accepting defeat.

Th is a combination of letters which Poe says occurs so often in our language that they can easily be picked out in a cipher of this length. How many times can a conjunction of two similar characters be found in the lines before us. .> .[-] occurs three times, which is often enough, perhaps, to establish the fact that they stand for *th*. Do I find them joined with a third character in the list of possible *thes*? Yes. .> [-] which would seem to fix both the *th* and the *e*.

But I have grown wary and must make myself sure. Do I find a word in which this combination of. > .[-] occurs twice, as sometimes happens with the *th* we are considering? No, but I find two other instances in which like contiguous symbols do appear twice in one word; the .< .[-] in No. 3 and the .V .)C in No. 4—a discovery the most embarrassing of all, since in both cases the symbols which begin the word are reversed at its end, as witness: .V .)C - - -)C .V — .< .[-] - - - .[-] .<. For, if .V)C stands for *th*, and the whole word showed in letters th- - -ht, which to any eye suggests the word *thought*, what does .< .[-] stand for, concerning which the same conditions are observable?

I could not answer. I had run on a snag.

Rules which applied to one part of the cipher failed in another. Could it be that a key was necessary to its proper solution? I began to think so, and, moreover, that Mrs. Packard had made use of some such help as I watched her puzzling in the window over these symbols. I recalled her movements, the length of time which elapsed before the cry of miserable understanding escaped her lips, the fact that her dress was torn apart at the throat when she came out, and decided that she had not only drawn some paper from her bosom helpful to the elucidation of these symbols, but that this paper was the one which had been the object of her frantic search the night I watched her shadow on the wall.

So convinced was I by these thoughts that any further attempt to solve the cryptogram without such aid as I have mentioned would end by leaving me where I was at present,—that is, in the fog,—that I allowed the lateness of the hour to influence me; and, putting aside my papers, I went to bed. If I had sat over them another hour, should I have been more fortunate? Make the attempt yourself and see.

CHAPTER XXII

MERCY

"Where is my wife?"

"Sleeping, sir, after a day of exhausting emotion."

"She didn't wire me?"

"No, sir."

"Perhaps she wasn't able?"

"She was not, Mayor Packard."

"I must see her. I came as soon as I could. Left Warner to fill my place on the platform, and it is the night of nights, too. Why, what's the matter?"

He had caught me staring over his shoulder at the form drawn up in the doorway.

"Nothing; I thought you had come alone."

"No, Mr. Steele is with me. He joined me at noon, just after I had telegraphed home. He has come back to finish the work I assigned him. He has at last discovered—or thinks he has—the real author of those libels. You have something special to say to me?" he whispered, as I followed him upstairs.

"Yes, and I think, if I were you, that I should say nothing to Mrs. Packard about Mr. Steele's having returned." And I rapidly detailed the occurrence of the afternoon, ending with Mrs. Packard's explanation to her servants.

The mayor showed impatience. "Oh, I can not bother with such nonsense as that," he declared; "the situation is too serious."

I thought so, too, when in another moment his wife's door opened and she stepped out upon the landing to meet him. Her eyes fell on Mr. Steele, standing at the foot of the stairs, before they encountered her husband; and though she uttered no cry and hardly paused in her approach toward the mayor, I saw the heart within her die as suddenly and surely as the flame goes out in a gust of wind.

"You!" There was hysteria in the cry. Pray God that the wild note in it was not that of incipient insanity! "How good of you to give up making your great speech to-night, just to see how I have borne this last outrage! You do see, don't you?" Here she drew her form to its full height. "My husband believes in me, and it gives me courage to face the whole world. Ah! is that Mr. Steele I see below there? Pardon me, Mr. Steele, if I show surprise. We heard a false report of your illness this afternoon. Henry, hadn't Mr. Steele better come up-stairs? I presume you are here to talk over this last dreadful paragraph with me."

"It is not necessary for Mr. Steele to join us if you do not wish him to," I heard the mayor whisper in his wife's ear.

"Oh, I do not mind," she returned with an indifference whose reality I probably gauged more accurately than he did.

"That is good." And he called Mr. Steele up. "You see she is reasonable enough," he muttered in my ear as he motioned me to follow them into the up-stairs sitting-room to which she had led the way. "The more heads the better in a discussion of this kind," was the excuse he gave his wife and Mr. Steele as he ushered me in.

As neither answered, I considered my presence accepted and sat down in as remote a corner as offered. Verily the fates were active in my behalf.

Mayor Packard was about to close the door, when Mrs. Packard suddenly leaped by him with the cry:

"There's the baby! She must have heard your voice." And rushing into the hall she came back with the child whom she immediately placed in its father's arms. Then she slowly seated herself. Not until she had done so did she turn to Mr. Steele.

"Sit," said she, with a look and gesture her husband would have marveled at had he not been momentarily occupied with the prattling child.

The secretary bowed and complied. Surely men of such great personal attractions are few. Instantly the light, shaded though it seemingly was in all directions, settled on his face, making him, to my astonished gaze, the leading personality in the group. Was this on account of the distinction inherent in extreme beauty or because of a new and dominating expression which had insensibly crept into his features?

The mayor, and the mayor only, seemed oblivious to the fact. Glancing up from the child, he opened the conference by saying: "Tell Mrs. Packard, Steele, what you have just told me."

With a quiet shifting of his figure which brought him into a better line with the woman he was asked to address, the secretary opened his lips to reply when she, starting, reached out one hand and drew toward herself the little innocent figure of her child, which she at once placed between herself and him. Seeing this, I recalled the scraps of cipher left in my room above and wished I had succeeded in determining their meaning, if only to understand the present enigmatical situation.

Meanwhile Mr. Steele was saying in the mellow tone of a man accustomed to tune his voice to suit all occasions: "Mrs. Packard will excuse me if I seem abrupt. In obedience to commands laid upon me by his Honor, I spent both Tuesday and Wednesday in inquiries as to the origin of the offensive paragraph which appeared in Monday's issue of the Leader. Names were given me, but too many of them. It took me two days to sift these down to one, and when I had succeeded in doing this, it was only to find that the man I sought was ninety miles away. Madam, I journeyed those ninety miles to learn that meanwhile he had returned to this city. While I was covering those miles for the second time, to-day's paragraph appeared. I hastened to accuse its author of libel, but the result was hardly what I expected. Perhaps you know what he said."

"No," she harshly returned, "I do not." And with the instinctive gesture of one awaiting attack she raised her now sleepy and nodding child in front of her laboring breast, with a look in her eyes which I see yet.

"He said—pardon me, your Honor, pardon me, Madam— that I was at liberty to point out what was false in it."

With a leap she was on her feet, towering above us all in her indignation and overpowering revolt against the man who was the conscious instrument of this insult. The child, loosened so suddenly from her arms, tottered and would have fallen, had not Mr. Steele leaned forward and drawn the little one across to himself. Mr. Packard, who, we must remember, had been more or less prepared for what his secretary had to say, cast a glance at his wife, teeming with varied emotions.

"And what did you reply to that?" were the words she hurled at the unabashed secretary.

"Nothing," was his grave reply. "I did not know myself what

was false in it."

With sudden faltering, Mrs. Packard reseated herself, while the mayor, outraged by what was evidently a very unexpected answer, leaned forward in great anger, crying:

"That was not the account you gave me of this wretched interview. Explain yourself, Mr. Steele. Don't you see that your silence at such a moment, to say nothing of the attitude you at present assume, is an insult to Mrs. Packard?"

The smile he met in reply was deprecatory enough; so were the words his outburst had called forth.

"I did not mean, and do not mean to insult Mrs. Packard. I am merely showing you how hampered a man is, whatever his feelings, when it comes to a question of facts known only to a lady with whom he has not exchanged fifty words since he came into her house. If Mrs. Packard will be good enough to inform me just how much and how little is true in the paragraph we are considering, I shall see this rascally reporter again and give him a better answer."

Mayor Packard looked unappeased. This was not the way to soothe a woman whom he believed to be greatly maligned. With an exclamation indicative of his feelings, he was about to address some hasty words to the composed, almost smiling, man who confronted him, when Mrs. Packard herself spoke with unexpected self-control, if not disdain.

"You are a very honest man, Mr. Steele. I commend the nicety of your scruples and am quite ready to trust myself to them. I own to no blot, in my past or present life, calling for public arraignment. If my statement of the fact is not enough, I here swear on the head of my child—"

"No, no," he quickly interpolated, "don't frighten the baby. Swearing is not necessary; I am bound to believe your word, Mrs. Packard." And lifting a sheet of paper from a pile lying on the table before him, he took a pencil from his pocket and began making lines to amuse the child dancing on his knee.

Mrs. Packard's eyes opened in wonder mingled with some emotion deeper than distaste, but she said nothing, only watched in a fascinated way his moving fingers. The mayor, mollified possibly by his secretary's last words, sank back again in his chair with the remark:

"You have heard Mrs. Packard's distinct denial. You are consequently armed for battle. See that you fight well. It is all a part of the scheme to break me up. One more paragraph of that kind and I shall be a wreck, even if my campaign is not."

"There will not be any more."

"Ah! you can assure me of that?"

"Positively."

"What are you playing there?" It was Mrs. Packard who spoke. She was pointing at the scribble he was making on the paper.

"Tit-tat-to," he smiled, "to amuse the baby."

Did she hate to see him so occupied, or was her own restlessness of a nature demanding a like outlet? Tearing her eyes away from him and the child, she looked about her in a wild way, till she came upon a box of matches standing on the large center-table around which they were all grouped. Taking some in her hand, she commenced to lay them out on the table before her, possibly in an attempt to attract the baby's attention to herself. Puerile business, but it struck me forcibly, possibly from the effect it appeared to have upon the mayor. Looking from one to the other in an astonishment which was not without its hint of some new and overmastering feeling on his own part, he remarked:

"Isn't it time for the baby to go to bed? Surely, our talk is too serious to be interrupted by games to please a child."

Without a word Mr. Steele rose and put the protesting child in the mother's arms. She, rising, carried it to the door, and, coming slowly back, reseated herself before the table and began to push the matches about again with fingers that trembled beyond her control. The mayor proceeded as if no time had elapsed since his last words.

"You had some words then with this Brainard—I think you called him Brainard—exacted some promise from him?"

"Yes, your Honor," was the only reply.

Did not Mrs. Packard speak, too? We all seemed to think so, for we turned toward her; but she gave no evidence of having said anything, though an increased nervousness was visible in her fingers as she pushed the matches about.

"I thought I was warranted in doing so much," continued Mr. Steele. "I could not buy the man with money, so I used threats."

"Right! anything to squelch him," exclaimed the mayor, but not with the vigor I expected from him. Some doubt, some dread—caught perhaps from his wife's attitude or expression—seemed to interpose between his indignation and the object of it. "You are our good friend, Steele, in spite of the shock you gave us a moment ago."

As no answer was made to this beyond a smile too subtle and too fine to be understood by his openhearted chief, the mayor proceeded to declare:

"Then that matter is at an end. I pray that it may have done us no real harm. I do not think it has. People resent attacks on women, especially, on one whose reputation has never known a shadow, as girl, wife, or mother."

"Yes," came in slow assent from the lips which had just smiled, and he glanced at Mrs. Packard whose own lips seemed suddenly to become dry, for I saw her try to moisten them as her right hand groped about for something on the tabletop and finally settled on a small paper-weight which she set down amongst her matches. Was it then or afterward that I began to have my first real doubt whether some shadow had not fallen across her apparently unsullied life?

"Yes, you are right," repeated Mr. Steele more energetically. "People do resent such insinuations against a woman, though I remember one case where the opposite effect was produced. It was when Collins ran for supervisor in Cleveland. He was a good fellow himself, and he had a wife who was all that was beautiful and charming, but who had once risked her reputation in an act which did call for public arraignment. Unfortunately, there was a man who knew of this act and he published it right and left and—"

"Olympia!" Mayor Packard was on his feet, pointing in sudden fury and suspicion at the table where the matches lay about in odd and, as I now saw, seemingly set figures. "You are doing something besides playing with those matches. I know Mr. Steele's famous cipher; he showed it to me a week ago; and so, evidently, do you, in spite of the fact that you have had barely fifty words with him since he came to the house. Let me read—ah!—give over that piece of paper you have there, Steele, if you would not have me think you as great a dastard as we know that Brainard to be!"

And while his wife drooped before his eyes and a cynical smile crept about the secretary's fine mouth, he caught up the sheet on which Steele had been playing tit-tat-to with the child, and glanced from the table to it and back again to the table on which the matches lay in the following device, the paper-weight answering for the dot:

7; L; .)7; [-]; ^V

Anna Katherine Green

"M," suddenly left the mayor's writing lips; then slowly, letter by letter, "E-R-C-Y. Mercy!" he vociferated. "Why does my wife appeal for mercy to you—a stranger—and in your own cipher! Miserable woman! What secret's here? Either you are—"

"Hush! some one's at the door!" admonished the secretary.

Mr. Packard turned quickly, and, smoothing his face rapidly, as such men must, started for the door. Mrs. Packard, flinging her whole soul into a look, met the secretary's eyes for a moment and then let her head sink forward on her hands above those telltale matches, from whose arrangement she had reaped despair in place of hope.

Mr. Steele smiled again, his fine, false smile, but after her head had fallen; not before. Indeed, he had vouchsafed no reply to her eloquent look. It was as if it had met marble till her eyes were bidden; then—

But Nixon was in the open doorway and Nixon was speaking:

"A telegram, your Honor."

The old man spoke briskly, even a little crisply—perhaps he always did when he addressed the mayor. But his eyes roamed eagerly and changed to a burning, red color when they fell upon the dejected figure of his mistress. I fancied that, had he dared, he would have leaped into the room and taken his own part—and who could rightly gage what that was?—in the scene which may have been far more comprehensive to him than to me. But he did not dare, and my eyes passed from him to the mayor.

"From Haines," that gentleman announced, forgetting the suggestive discovery he had just made in the great and absorbing interest of his campaign. "'Speech good—great applause becoming thunderous at flash of your picture. All right so far if—'" he read out, ceasing abruptly at the "if" which, as I afterward understood, really ended the message. "No answer," he explained to Nixon as he hurriedly, dismissed him. "That 'if' concerns you," he now declared, coming back to his wife and to his troubles at the same instant. "Explain the mystery which seems likely to undo me. Why do you sit there bowed under my accusations? Why should Henry Packard's wife cry for mercy, to any man? Because those damnable accusations are true? Because you have a secret in your past and this man knows it?"

Slowly she rose, slowly she met his eyes, and even he started back at her pallor and the drawn misery in her face. But she did not speak. Instead of that she simply reached out and laid her hand on Mr. Steele's arm, drooping almost to the ground as she did so. "Mercy!" she suddenly wailed, but this time to the man who had so relentlessly accused her. The effect was appalling. The mayor reeled, then sprang forward with his hand outstretched for his secretary's throat. But his words were for his wife. "What does this mean? Why do you take your stand by the side of another man than myself? What have I done or what have you done that I should live to face such an abomination as this?"

It was Steele who answered, with a lift of his head as full of assertion as it was of triumph.

"You? nothing; she? everything. You do not know this woman, Mayor Packard; for instance, you do not know her name."

"Not know her name? My wife's?"

"Not in the least. This lady's name is Brainard. So is mine. Though she has lived with you several years in ignorance of my continued existence, no doubt, she is my wife and not yours. We were married in Boone, Minnesota, six years ago."

Anna Katherine Green

CHAPTER XXIII

THE WIFE'S TALE

Ten minutes later this woman was pleading her cause. She had left the side of the man who had just assumed the greatest of all rights over her and was standing in a frenzy of appeal before him she loved so deeply and yet had apparently wronged.

Mayor Packard was sitting with his head in his hands in the chair into which he had dropped when the blow fell which laid waste his home, his life, the future of his child and possibly the career which was as much, perhaps more, to him than all these. He had not uttered a word since that dreadful moment. To all appearance her moans of contrition fell upon deaf ears, and she had reached the crisis of her misery without knowing the extent of the condemnation hidden in his persistent silence. Collapse seemed inevitable, but I did not know the woman or the really wonderful grip she held on herself. Seeing that he was moved by nothing she had said, she suddenly paused, and presently I heard her observe in quite a different tone:

"There is one thing you must know—which I thought you would know without my telling you. I have never lived with this man, and I believed him dead when I gave my hand to you."

The mayor's fingers twitched. She had touched him at last. "Speak! tell me," he murmured hoarsely. "I do not want to do you any injustice."

"I shall have to begin far, far back; tell about my early life and all its temptations," she faltered, "or you will never understand."

"Speak."

Sensible at this point of the extreme impropriety of my presence, I rose, with an apology, to leave. But she shook her head quickly, determinedly, saying that as I had heard so much I must hear more. Then she went on with her story.

"I have committed a great fault," said she, "but one not so deep or inexcusable as now appears, whatever that man may say," she added with a slow turn toward the silent secretary.

Did she expect to provoke a reply from the man who, after the first triumphant assertion of his claim, had held himself as removed from her and as unresponsive to her anguish as had he whom she directly addressed? If so, she must have found her disappointment bitter, for he did not respond with so much as a look. He may have smiled, but if so, it was not a helpful smile; for she turned away with a shudder and henceforth faced and addressed the mayor only.

"My mother married against the wishes of all her family and they never forgave her. My father died early—he had never got on in the world—and before I was fifteen I became the sole support of my invalid mother as well as of myself. We lived in Boone, Minnesota.

"You can imagine what sort of support it was, as I had no special talent, no training and only the opportunity given by a crude western town of two or three hundred inhabitants. I washed dishes in the hotel kitchen—I who had a millionaire uncle in Detroit and had been fed on tales of wealth and culture by a mother who remembered her own youth and was too ignorant of my real nature to see the harm she was doing. I washed dishes and ate my own heart out in shame and longing—bitter shame and frenzied longing, which you must rate at their full force if you would know my story and how I became linked to this man.

"I was sixteen when we first met. He was not then what he is now, but he was handsome enough to create an excitement in town and to lift the girl he singled out into an enviable prominence. Unfortunately, I was that girl. I say unfortunately, because his good looks failed to arouse in me more than a passing admiration; and in accepting his attentions, I consulted my necessities and pride rather than the instincts of my better nature. When he asked me to marry him I recoiled. I did not know why then, nor did I know why later; but know why now. However, I let this premonition pass and engaged myself to him, and the one happy moment I knew was when I told my mother what I had done, and saw her joy and heard the hope with which she impulsively cried: 'It is something I can write your uncle. Who knows? Perhaps he may forgive me my marriage when he hears that my child is going to do so well!' Poor mother! she had felt the glamour of my lover's good looks and cleverness much more than I had. She saw from indications to which I was blind that I was going to marry a man of mark, and was much more interested in the possible reply she might receive to the letter with which she had broken the silence of years between herself and her family than in the marriage itself.

"But days passed, a week, and no answer came. My uncle—the only relative remaining in which we could hope to awaken any interest, or rather, the only one whose interest would be worth awakening, he being a millionaire and unmarried—declined, it appeared, any communication with one so entirely removed from his sympathies; and the disappointment of it broke my mother's heart. Before my wedding-day came she was lying in the bare cemetery I had passed so often with a cold dread in my young and bounding heart.

"With her loss the one true and unselfish bond which held me to my lover was severed, and, unknown to him—(perhaps he hears it now for the first time)—I had many hours of secret hesitation which might have ended in a positive refusal to marry him if I had not been afraid of his anger and the consequences of an open break. With all his protestations of affection and the very ardent love he made me, he had not succeeded in rousing my affections, but he had my fears. I knew that to tell him to his face I would not marry him would mean death to him and possibly to myself. Such intuition, young as I was, did I have of his character, though I comprehended so little the real range of his mind and the unswerving trend of his ambitious nature.

"So my, wedding-day came and we were united in the very hotel where I had so long served in a menial capacity. The social distinctions in such a place being small and my birth and breeding really placing me on a par with my employer and his family, I was given the parlor for this celebration and never, never, shall I forget its mean and bare look, even to my untutored eyes; or how lonely those far hills looked, through the small-paned window I faced; or what a shadow seemed to fall across them as the parson uttered those fateful words, so terrible to one whose heart is not in them: What God hath joined together let no man put asunder. Death and not life awaited me on that bleak hillside, or so I thought, though the bridegroom at my side was the handsomest man I had ever seen and had rather exceeded than failed in his devotion to me as a lover.

"The ceremony over, I went up-stairs to make my final preparations for departure. No bridesmaids or real friends had lent joy to the occasion; and when I closed that parlor door upon my bridegroom and the two or three neighbors and boon companions with whom he was making merry, I found myself alone with my dead heart and a most unwelcome future. I remember, as the lock clicked and the rude hall, ruder even than the wretched half-furnished room I had just left, opened before me, a sensation of terror at leaving even this homely refuge and a half-formed wish that I was going back to my dish-washing in the kitchen. It was therefore with a shock, which makes my brain reel yet, that I saw, lying on a little table which I had to pass, a letter directed to myself, bearing the postmark, Detroit. What might there not be in it? What? What?

"Gasping as much with fear as delight, I caught up the letter, and, rushing with it to my room, locked myself in and tore open the envelope. A single sheet fell out; it was signed with the name I had heard whispered in my ear from early childhood, and always in connection with riches and splendor and pleasures,—it was rapture to dream of. This was an agitation in itself, but the words—the words! I have never told them to mortal being, but I must tell them now; I remember them as I remember the look of my child's face when she was first put in my arms, the child—"

She had underrated her strength. She broke into a storm of weeping which shook to the very soul one of the two men who listened to her, though he made no move to comfort her or allay it. The alienation thus expressed produced its effect, and, stricken deeper than the fount of tears, she suddenly choked back every sob and took up the thread of her narrative with the calmness born of despair,

"These were the words, these and no others:

"'If my niece will break all ties and come to me completely unhampered, she may hope to find a permanent home in my house and a close hold upon my affections.

IRA T. HOUGHTALING.'

"Unhampered! with the marriage-vow scarcely cold on my lips! Without tie! and a husband waiting below to take me to his home on the hillside—a hillside so bare and bleak that the sight of it had sent a shudder to my heart as the wedding ring touched my finger. The irony of the situation was more than I could endure, and alone, with my eyes fixed on the comfortless heavens, showing gray and cold through the narrow panes of my windows, I sank to the floor insensible.

"When I came to myself I was still alone, and the twilight a little more pronounced than when my misery had turned it to blackest midnight. Rising, I read that letter again, and, plainly as the acknowledgment betrays the selfishness lying at the basis of my character, the temptation which thereupon seized me had never an instant of relenting or one conscientious scruple to combat it. I simply, at that stage in my life and experience, could not do otherwise than I did. Saying to myself that vows, as empty of heart as mine, were void before God and man, I sat down and wrote a few words to the man whose step on the stair I dreaded above everything else in the world; and, leaving the note on the table, unlocked my door and looked out. The hall connecting with my room was empty, but not so the lower one. There I could hear voices and laughter, Mr. Brainard's loud above all the rest,—a fatal sound to me, cutting off all escape in that direction. But another way offered and that one near at hand. Communicating with the very hall in which I stood was an outside staircase running down to the road—a means of entering and leaving a house which I never see now wherever I may encounter it, without a gush of inward shame and terror, so instinctive and so sharp that I have never been able to hide it from any one whose eye might chance to be upon me at the moment. But that night I was conscious of no shame, barely of any terror, only of the necessity for haste. The train on which I was determined to fly was due in a little less than an hour at a station two miles down the road.

"That I should be followed farther than the turbulent stream which crossed the road only a quarter of a mile from the hotel, I did not fear. For in the hurried note I had left behind me, I had bidden them to look for me there, saying that I had been precipitate in marrying one I did not really love, and, overcome by a sense of my mistake, I was resolved on death.

"A lie! but what was a lie to me then, who saw in my life with this man an amelioration of my present state, but an amelioration only, while in the prospects held out to me by my uncle I foresaw not only release from a hated union, but every delight which my soul had craved since my mother could talk

Anna Katherine Green

to me of wealth and splendor.

"Behold me, then, stealing down the side of the house in a darkness which during the last few minutes had become impenetrable. A shadow, where all was shadowy, I made for the woods and succeeded in reaching their shelter just as there rose in the distance behind me that most terrible of all sounds to a woman's ear, a man's loud cry of anguish and rage."

She was not looking at that man now, but I was. As these words left her lips, Mr. Steele's hand crept up and closed over his heart, though his face was like that of a marble image set in immovable lines. I feared him, I admired him, and found myself still looking at him as she went gaspingly on:

"Reckless of the dangers of the road, fearing nothing but what pressed upon me from behind, I flew straight for the stream, on whose verge I meant then to stop, and, having by some marvel of good luck or Providence reached it without a mishap, I tore the cloak from my shoulders, and, affixing one end to the broken edge of the bridge, flung the other into the water. Then with one loud ear-piercing shriek thrown back on the wind—see! I tell all—I leave out nothing—I fled away in the direction of the station.

"For some reason I had great confidence in the success of this feint and soon was conscious of but one fear, and that was being recognized by the station-master, who knew my face and figure even if he did not know my new city-made dress. So when I had made sure by the clock visible from the end window that I was in ample time for the expected train, I decided to remain in the dark at the end of the platform till the cars were about starting, and then to jump on and buy my ticket from the conductor.

"But I never expected such an interminable wait. Minute after minute went by without a hint of preparation for the advancing train. The hour for leaving arrived, passed, and not a man had shown himself on the platform. Had a change been made in the time-table? If so, what a prospect lay before me! Autumn nights are chill in Minnesota, and, my cloak having been sacrificed, I found poor protection in my neat but far from warm serge dress. However, I did not fully realize my position till another passenger arrived late and panting, and I heard some one shout out to him from the open door that an accident had occurred below and that it would be five hours at least before the train would come through.

"Five hours! and no shelter in sight save the impossible one of the station itself. How could I pass away that time! How endure the cold and fatigue? By pacing to and fro in the road? I tried it, resolutely tried it, for an hour, then a new terror, a new suspense, gripped me, and I discovered that I could never live through the hours; never, in fact, take the train when it came without knowing what had happened in Boone and whether the feint on which I relied had achieved its purpose. There was time to steal back, time to see and hear what would satisfy me of my own safety; and then to have some purpose in my movement! How much better than this miserable pacing back and forth just to start the stagnating blood and make the lagging moments endurable!

"So I turned again toward Boone. I was not in the mood to fear darkness or any encounter save one, and experienced hesitation only when I found myself reapproaching the bridge. Shadows which had protected me until now failed me there, and it was with caution I finally advanced and emerged upon the open spot where the road crossed the river. But even this was not needed. In the wide stretch before me cut by the inky stream, I saw no signs of life, and it was not till I was on the bridge itself that I discerned in the black hollows below the glint of a lantern, lighting up the bending forms of two or three men who were dragging at something which heaved under their hands with the pull of the stream.

"It was a sight which has never left me, but one which gave wings to my feet that night and sent me flying on till a fork in the road brought me to a standstill. To the left lay the hotel. I could see its windows glimmering with faint lights, while, away to the right, there broke upon me from the hillside a solitary sparkle; but this sparkle came from the house where, but for the letter hidden in my heart, I should be sitting at this moment before my own fireside.

"What moved me? God knows. It may have been duty; it may have been curiosity; it may have been only dread to know the worst and know it at once; but seeing that single gleam I began to move toward it, and, before I was aware, I had reached the house, edged up to its unshaded window and taken a frightened look within.

"I was prepared and yet unprepared for what I saw. Within, standing alone, with garments dripping, gazing in frenzy at a slip of paper which clung wet about his hand, stood my husband. My words to him! I could see it in his eyes and the desperation which lit up all his features.

"Drawing back in terror from the road, I watched him fling that letter of from his fingers as he would a biting snake, and, striding to a cupboard high up on the wall, take down something I could not see and did not guess at till the sharp sound of a pistol-shot cleft my ear, and I beheld him fall face downward on the carpet of fresh autumn leaves with which he had hidden the bare floor in expectation of his bride.

"The shriek which involuntarily went up from my lips must have rung far and wide, but only the groaning of the night-wind answered me. Driven by my fears to do something to save him if he was not yet dead, I tried the door, but it was locked; so was the window. Yet I might have battered my way in at that moment had I not heard two men coming down the road, one of whom was shouting to the other: 'I did not like his face. I shan't sleep till I've seen him again.'"

"Somewhat relieved, I drew back from the road, but did not quit the spot till those men, seeing through the window what had happened, worked their way in and lifted him up in their arms. The look with which they let him fall back again was eloquent, and convinced me that it was death I saw. I started again upon my shuddering flight from Boone, secure in the belief that while my future would surely hold remorse for me, it would nevermore burden me with a hindrance in the shape of an unloved husband."

CHAPTER XXIV

THE SINS OF THE FATHERS

The suspense which had held us tense and speechless was for the moment relieved and Mr. Steele allowed himself the following explanation:

"My hand trembled and the bullet penetrated an inch too high."

Then he relapsed again into silence.

Mrs. Packard shuddered and went on:

"It may seem incredible to you, it seems incredible now to myself, but I completed my journey, entered my uncle's house, was made welcome there and started upon my new life without letting my eyes fall for one instant on the columns of a newspaper. I did not dare to see what they contained. That short but bitter episode of my sixteenth year was a nightmare of horror, to be buried with my old name and all that could interfere with the delights of the cultured existence which my uncle's means and affection opened before me. Two years and I hardly remembered; three years and it came to me only in dreams; four and even dreams failed to suggest it; the present, the glorious present was all. I had met you, Henry, and we had loved and married.

"Did any doubts come to disturb my joy? Very few. I had

never received a word from Minnesota. I was as dead to every one there as they all were to me. I believed myself free and that the only wrong I did was in not taking you into my confidence. But this, the very nature of my secret forbade. How could I tell you what would inevitably alienate your affections? That act of my early girlhood by which I had gained an undeserved freedom had been too base; sooner than let you know this blot on my life, I was content to risk the possibility—the inconceivable possibility—of Mr. Brainard's having survived the attack he had made upon his own life. Can you understand such temerity? I can not, now that I see its results before me.

"So the die was cast and I became a wife instead of the mere shadow of one. You were prosperous, and not a sorrow came to disturb my sense of complete security till that day two weeks ago, when, looking up in my own library, I saw, gleaming between me and the evening lamp, a face, which, different as it was in many respects, tore my dead past out of the grave and sent my thoughts reeling back to a lonely road on a black hillside with a lighted window in view, and behind that window the outstretched form of a man with his head among leaves not redder than his blood.

"I have said to you, I have said to others, that a specter rose upon me that day in the library. It was such to me,—an apparition and nothing else. Perhaps he meant to impress himself as such, for I had heard no footfall and only looked up because of the constraining force of the look which awaited me. I knew afterward that it was a man whom I had seen, a man whom you yourself had introduced into the house; but at the instant I thought it a phantom of my forgotten past sent to shock and destroy me; and, struck speechless with the horror of it, I lost that opportunity of mutual explanation which might have saved me an unnecessary and cruel experience. For this man, who recognized me more surely than I did him, who perhaps knew who I was before he ever entered my house, has sported for two weeks with my fears and hopes as a tiger with his prey. Maintaining his attitude of stranger—you have been

Anna Katherine Green

witness to his manner in my presence—he led me slowly but surely to believe myself deceived by an extraordinary resemblance; a resemblance, moreover, which did not hold at all times, and which frequently vanished altogether, as I recalled the straight-featured but often uncouth aspect of the man who had awakened the admiration of Boone. Memory had been awakened and my sleep filled with dreams, but the unendurable had been spared me and I was thanking God with my whole heart, when suddenly one night, when an evening spent with friends in the old way had made me feel safe, my love safe, my husband and my child safe, there came to my ears from below the sound of a laugh, loud, coarse and deriding,—such a laugh as could spring from no member of my own household, such a laugh as I heard but once before and that in the by-gone years when some one asked Mr. Brainard if he meant to live always in Boone. The shock was terrible, and when I learned that the secretary, and the secretary only, was below, I knew who that secretary was and yielded to the blow.

"Yet hope dies hard with the happy. I knew, but it was not enough to know,—I must be sure. There was a way—it came to me with my first fluttering breath as I recovered from my faint. In those old days when I was thrown much with this man, he had shown me a curious cipher and taught me how to use it. It was original with himself, he said, and some day we might be glad of a method of communication which would render our correspondence inviolable. I could not see why he considered this likely ever to be desirable, but I took the description of it which he gave me and promised that I would never let it leave my person. I even allowed him to solder about my neck the chain which held the locket in which he had placed it. Consequently I had it with me when I fled from Boone, and for the first few weeks after arriving at my uncle's house in Detroit. Then, wishing to banish every reminder of days I was so anxious to forget, I broke that chain, destroyed the locket and hid away from every one's sight the now useless and despised cipher. Why I retained the cipher I can not explain. Now, that cipher must prove my salvation. If I could find it again I was sure that the shock of receiving from my hand certain words written in the symbols he had himself taught me would call from him an involuntary revelation. I should know what I had to fear. But so many changes had taken place and so long a time elapsed since I hid this slip of paper away that I was not even sure I still retained it; but after spending a good share of the night in searching for it, I finally came across it in one of my old trunks.

"The next morning I made my test. Perhaps, Henry, you remember my handing Mr. Steele an empty envelope to mail which he returned with an air of surprise so natural and seemingly unfeigned that he again forced me to believe that he was the stranger he appeared. Though he must have recognized at a glance—for he was an adept in this cipher once—the seven simple symbols in which I had expressed the great cry of my soul 'Is it you?' he acted the innocent secretary so perfectly that all my old hopes returned and I experienced one hour of perfect joy. Then came another reaction. Letty brought in the baby with a paper pinned to her coat. She declared to us that a woman had been the instrument of this outrage, though the marks inside, suggesting the cipher but with characteristic variations bespeaking malice, could only have been made by one hand.

"How I managed to maintain sufficient hold upon my mind to drag the key from my breast and by its means to pick out the meaning of the first three words—words which once read suggested all the rest—I can not now imagine. Death was in my heart and the misery of it all more than human strength could bear; yet I compared paper with paper carefully, intelligently, till these words from the prayer- book with all their threatening meaning to me and mine started into life before me: 'Visiting the sins—' Henry, you know the words 'Visiting the sins of the fathers upon the children unto the third and fourth generation.' Upon the children! Henry, he meant Laura! our little Laura! I had wakened vengeance in a fiend. The man who had calmly smiled in my face as he handed me back that empty envelope inscribed with the wild appeal, 'Is it you?' was the man I had once driven to the verge of the grave and who had come back now to destroy us all.

"Yet, such is the reaching out of the drowning for straws, I did not utterly despair till Nixon brought me from this man's lodging-house, where I had sent him, a specimen of his handwriting.

"Nixon is the only confidant I have had. Nixon knew me as a girl when he worked in my uncle's home, and has always had the most unbounded, I may say jealous, affection for me. To him I had dared impart that I did not trust your new secretary; that he looked like a man I once knew who was a determined opponent of the party now trying to elect you; that a specimen of his writing would make me quite sure, and begged him to get it. I thought he might pick up such in the little office below, but he was never able to do so—Mr. Steele has taken care not to leave a line written in this house—but he did find a few lines signed with his name in his own room at the boarding-house, and these he showed me before he told me the result of his errand. They settled all doubts. What is to be my fate? Surely this man has no real claim on me, after all these years, when I thought myself your true and honest wife. He may ruin your campaign, defeat your hopes, overwhelm me with calumny and a loss of repute, but surely, surely he can not separate us. The law will not uphold him in that; will it, Henry? Say that it will not, say—oh, say that—it—will not—do—that, or we shall live to curse the day, not when we were born; but when our little innocent child came to us!"

CHAPTER XXV

THE FINGER ON THE WALL

At this appeal the mayor rose and faced his secretary and the spectacle was afforded me of seeing two strong men drawn up in conflict over a woman both had cherished above all else. And it was characteristic of the forceful men, as well as the extreme nature of the conflict, that both were quiet in manner and speech—perhaps the mayor the more so, as he began the struggle by saying:

"Is what Mrs. Packard says of your playing with her fears during these two weeks true, Mr. Steele?"

Without a droop of his eye, or a tremor in his voice, the answer came short, sharp and emphatic:

"Yes."

"Then, you are a villain! and I shall not feel myself called upon to show you any consideration beyond what justice demands. Have you any plea to urge beyond the natural one of her seemingly unprovoked desertion of you? Has not my wife—" the nobility with which he emphasized those two words made my heart swell—"spoken the truth?"

Ah! then the mask of disdainful serenity with which the other had hitherto veiled the burning anguish of his soul fell in one burst of irresistible passion.

"True! yes, it is true. But what does that truth involve for me? Not two weeks, but seven years of torture, five of them devoted to grief for her, loss, and two to rage and bitter revulsion against her whole sex when I found her alive, and myself the despised victim of her deception."

"She wronged you—she acknowledges that—but it was the wrong of an unthinking child—not of a realizing woman. Would you, a realizing man, tear her now from home, from her child, from her place in the community and my heart— make her despicable as well as unhappy, just to feed your revenge?"

"Yes, I would do that."

"Jeopardize interests you have so often professed in my hearing to be far above personal consideration—the success of your party, the triumph of your political principles?"

"My political principles!" Oh, the irony of his voice, the triumph in his laugh! "And what do you know of them? What I have said. Mayor Packard, your education as a politician has yet to be completed before you will be fit for the governorship of a state. I am an adept at the glorification of the party, of the man that it suits my present exigencies to promote, but it is a faculty which should have made you pause before you trusted me with the furtherance and final success of a campaign which may outlast those exigencies. I have not always been of your party; I am not so now at heart."

The mayor, outraged in every sentiment of honor as well as in the most cherished feelings of his heart, lowered upon his unmoved secretary with a wrath which would have borne down any other man before it.

"Do you mean to say, you, that your work is a traitor's work? That the glorification you speak of is false? That you may talk in my favor, but that when you come to the issue, you will vote according to your heart; that is, for Stanton?"

"I have succeeded in making myself intelligible."

The mayor flushed; indignation gave him vehemence.

"Then," he cried, "I take back the word by which I qualified you a moment ago. You are not a villain, you are a dastard."

Mr. Steele bowed in a way which turned the opprobrium into a seeming compliment.

"I have suffered so many wrongs at your hands that I can not wonder at suffering this one more."

Then slowly and with a short look at her: "The woman who has queened it so long in C—society can not wish to undergo the charge of bigamy?"

"You will bring such a charge?"

"Certainly, if she does not voluntarily quit her false position, and, accepting the protection of the man whose name is really hers, go from this house at once."

At this alternative, uttered with icy deliberation, Mrs. Packard recoiled with a sharp cry; but the mayor thrust a sudden sarcastic query at his opponent:

"Which name? Steele or Brainard? You acknowledged both."

"My real name is Brainard; therefore, it is also hers. But I shall be content if she will take my present one of Steele. More than that, I shall be content if she will honestly accept from my hands a place of refuge where I swear she shall remain unmolested by me till this matter can be legally settled. I do not wish to make myself hateful to her, for I anticipate the day when she will be my wife in heart as she is now in law."

"Never!"

The word rang out in true womanly revolt. "I will die before that day ever comes to separate me from the man I love and the child who calls me mother. You may force me from this house, you may plunge me into poverty, into contumely, but you shall never make me look upon myself as other than the wife of this good man, whom I have wronged but will never disgrace."

"Madam," declared the inflexible secretary with a derisive appreciation which bowed her once proud head upon her shamed breast, "you are all I thought you when I took you from Crabbe's back-pantry in Boone to make you the honor and glory of a life which I knew then, as well as I do now, would not long run in obscure channels."

It was a sarcasm calculated to madden the proud man who, only a few minutes before, had designated the object of it by the sacred name of wife. But beyond a hasty glance at the woman it had bowed almost to the ground, the mayor gave no evidence of feeling either its force or assumption. Other thoughts were in his mind than those roused by jealous anger. "How old were you then?" he demanded with alarming incongruity. The secretary started. He answered, however, calmly enough:

"I? Seven years ago I was twenty-five. I am thirty-two now."

"So I have heard you say. A man of twenty-five is old enough to have made a record, Mr. Steele—" The mayor's tone hardened, so did his manner; and I saw why he had been such a power in the courts before he took up politics and an office. "Mr. Steele, I do not mean you to disturb my house or to rob me of my wife. What was your life before you met Olympia Brewster?"

A pause, the slightest in the world,—but the keen eye of the astute lawyer noted it, and his tone grew in severity and assurance. "You have known for two years that this woman whom you called yours was within your reach, if not under your very eye, and you forbore to claim her. Has this delay had anything to do with the record of those years to which I have just alluded?"

Had the random shot told? The secretary's eye did not falter, nor his figure lose an inch of its height, yet the impression made by his look and attitude were not the same; the fire had gone out of them; a blight had struck his soul—the flush of his triumph was gone.

Mayor Packard was merciless.

"Only two considerations could hold back a man like you from urging a claim he regarded as a sacred right; the fact of a former marriage or the remembrance of a forfeited citizenship—pardon me, we can not mince matters in a strait like this—which would delegalize whatever contract you may have entered into."

Still the secretary's eye did not swerve, though he involuntarily stretched forth his hand toward the table as if afraid of betraying a tremor in his rigidly drawn-up figure.

"Was there the impediment of a former marriage?"

No answer from the sternly set lips.

"Or was it that you once served a term—a very short term, cut short by a successful attempt at escape in a Minnesota prison?"

"Insults!" broke from those set lips and nothing more.

"Mr. Steele, I practised law in that state for a period of three years. All the records of the office and of the prison register are open to me. Over which of them should I waste my time?"

Then the tiger broke loose in the man who from the aggressor had become the attacked, and he cried:

"I shall never answer; the devil has whispered his own suggestions in your ear; the devil and nothing else."

But the mayor, satisfied that he made his point, smiled calmly, saying:

"No, not the devil, but yourself. You, even the you of seven years back, would not have lived in any country town if necessity, or let us say, safety, had not demanded it. You, with your looks and your ambitions,—to marry at twenty-five a girl from the kitchen! any girl, even if she had the making of an Olympia Packard, if you did not know that it was in your power to shake her off when you got ready to assert yourself, or better prospects offered? The cipher and the desirability you expressed of a means of communication unreadable save by you two,—all this was enough to start the suspicion; your own manner has done the rest. Mr. Steele, you are both a villain and a bastard, and have no right in law to this woman. Contradict me if you dare."

"I dare, but will not," was the violent reply. "I shall not give you even that satisfaction. This woman who has gone through the ceremony of marriage with both of us shall never know to which of us she is the legal wife. Perhaps it is as good a revenge as the other. It certainly will interfere as much with her peace."

"Oh, oh, not that! I can not bear that!" leaped in anguish from her lips. "I am a pure woman, let no such torture be inflicted upon me. Speak! tell the truth as you are the son of a woman you would have us believe honest."

A smile then, cold but alive with gloating triumph, altered the straight line of his lips for an instant as he advanced toward the door. "A woman over the possession of whom it is an honor to quarrel!" were his words as he passed the mayor with a bow.

I looked to see the mayor spring and grasp him by the throat, but that was left for another hand. As the secretary bent to touch the door it suddenly flew violently open and Nixon, quivering in every limb and with his face afire, sprang in and seized upon the other with a violence of passion which would have been deadly had there been any strength behind it.

It was but child's play for so strong a man as Mr. Steele to shake off so futile a grasp, and he did so with a rasping laugh. But the next moment he was tottering, blanched and helpless, and while struggling to right himself and escape, yielded more and more to a sudden weakness sapping his life-vigor, till he fell prone and apparently lifeless on the lounge toward which, with a final effort, he had thrown himself.

"Good! Good!" rang thrilling through the room, as the old man reeled back from the wall against which he had been cast. "God has finished what these old arms had only strength enough to begin. He is dead this time, and it's a mercy! Thank God, Miss Olympia! thank God as I do now on my knees!" But here catching the mayor's eye, he faltered to his feet again, saying humbly as he crept away:

"I couldn't help it, your Honor. I shouldn't have been listening at the door; but I have loved Miss Olympia, as we used to call her, more than anything in the world ever since she came to make my old master's house a place of sunshine, and all I'm sorry for is that God had to do the finishing which twenty years ago I could have done myself."

CHAPTER XXVI

"BITTER AS THE GRAVE"

But Nixon was wrong. Mr. Steele did not die—not this time. Cared for by the physician who had been hastily summoned, he slowly but surely revived and by midnight was able to leave the house. As he passed the mayor on his way out, I heard Mr. Packard say:

"I shall leave the house myself in a few minutes. I do not mean that your disaffection shall ruin my campaign any more than I mean to leave a stone unturned to substantiate my accusation that you had no right to marry and possess legal claims over the woman whose happiness you have endeavored to wreck. If you are wise you will put no further hindrance in my way."

I heard no answer, for at that instant a figure appeared in the open door which distracted all our attention. Miss Thankful, never an early sleeper and much given, as we know, to looking out of her window, had evidently caught the note of disaster from the coming and going of the doctor. She had run in from next door and now stood panting in the open doorway face to face with Mr. Steele, with her two hands held out, in one of which, remarkable as it seems to relate, I saw the package of bonds which I had been fortunate enough to find for her.

The meeting seemed to paralyze both; her face which had been full of tremulous feeling blanched and hardened, while he, stopped in some speech or final effort he was about to make, yielded to the natural brutality which underlay his polished exterior, and, in an access of rage which almost laid him prostrate again, lifted his arm and struck her out of his path. As she reeled to one side the bonds flew from her hand and lay at his feet; but he saw nothing; he was already half-way down the walk and in another moment the bang of his carriage door announced his departure.

The old lady, muttering words I could not hear, stared mute and stricken at the bonds which the mayor had hastened to lift and place in her hands.

Pitying her and anxious to relieve him from the embarrassment of her presence when his own mind and heart were full of misery, I rushed down to her side and endeavored to lead her away. She yielded patiently enough to my efforts, but, as she turned away, she cast one look at the mayor and with the tears rolling down her long and hollow cheeks murmured in horror and amaze:

"He struck me!"

The flash in Mayor Packard's eye showed sympathy, but the demands of the moment were too great for him to give to those pathetic words the full significance which I suddenly suspected them to hold. As I led her tottering figure down the step and turned toward her door I said gently:

"Who was the man? Who was it that struck you?"

She answered quickly and with broken-hearted emphasis "My nephew! my sister's son, and I had come to give him all our money. We have waited three days for him to come to us. We thought he would when he knew the bonds had been found, but he never came near, never gave us a chance to enrich him; and when I heard he was ill and saw the carriage which had come to take him away, we could not stand it another minute and so I ran out and—and he struck me! looked in my face and struck me!"

I folded her in my arms, there and then at the foot of her own doorstep, and when I felt her heart beating on mine, I whispered:

"Bless God for it! He has a hard and cruel heart, and would make no good use of this money. Live to spend it as your brother desired, to make over the old house and reinstate the old name. He would not have wished it wasted on one who must have done you cruel wrong, since he has lived so many days beside you without showing his interest in you or even acknowledging your relationship."

"There were reasons," she protested, gently withdrawing herself, but holding me for a minute to her side. "He has had great fortune—is a man of importance now—we did not wish to interfere with his career. It was only after the money was found that we felt he should come. We should not have asked him to take back his old name, we should simply have given him what he thought best to take and been so happy and proud to see him. He is so handsome and fortunate that we should not have begrudged it, if he had taken it all. But he struck me! he struck me! He will never get a dollar now."

Relieved, for the natural good sense of the woman was reasserting itself, I gave her hands a squeeze and quickly ran back to where the mayor was holding the door for me.

"She is all right now," I remarked, as I slid by him upstairs; and that was all I said. The rest must wait a more auspicious moment—the moment when he really would have time to take up the gage which Mr. Steele had thrown down to him in his final words.

I was not a witness to the parting interview between Mayor Packard and his wife; I had stolen into the nursery, for a look at the little one. I found her sleeping sweetly, with one chubby hand under her rounded cheek. Thus had she lain and thus had she slept during all those dreadful minutes, when her future hung, trembling in the balance.

CHAPTER XXVII

A CHILD'S PLAYTHINGS

I was too much overwhelmed by all these events to close my eyes that night. The revelation of Mr. Steele's further duplicity, coming so immediately upon the first, roused fresh surmises and awakened thoughts which soon set my wits working in a direction as new as it was unexpected. I had believed my work over in this house, but as I recalled all the occurrences of the evening and turned the situation, as it now confronted me, over and over in my mind, I felt that it had just begun. There must be something in this latest development to help us in the struggle which lay before us. The rage which sprang up in him as he confronted his old aunt at this moment of his triumphant revenge argued a weakness in his armor which it might yet be my part to discover and reveal. I knew Mrs. Packard well enough to realize that the serenity into which she had fallen was a fictitious serenity, and must remain so as long as any doubt remained of the legality of the tie uniting her to this handsome fiend. Were the means suggested by the mayor of promising enough character to accomplish the looked-for end?

I remembered the man's eyes as the mayor let fall his word of powerful threat, and doubted it. Once recovered from the indisposition which now weakened him, he would find means to thwart any attempts made by Mayor Packard to undermine the position he had taken as the legal husband of Olympia— sufficiently so, at least, to hinder happiness between the pair whose wedded life he not only envied but was determined to break up, unless some flaw in his past could be discovered through Miss Quinlan—the aunt whose goodness he had slighted and who now seemed to be in a frame of mind to help our cause if its pitiful aspects were once presented to her. I resolved to present the case without delay. Morning came at last, and I refreshed myself as well as I could, and, after a short visit to Mrs. Packard's bedside during which my purpose grew with every moment I gazed down on her brave but pitiful face, put on my hat and jacket and went next door.

I found the two old ladies seated in their state apartment making calculations. At sight of my face they both rose and the "O my dear" from Miss Charity and the "God bless you, child," from Miss Thankful showed that both hearts were yet warm. Gradually I introduced the topic of their nephew; gradually I approached the vital question of the disgrace.

The result upset all my growing hopes. He had never told them just what the disgrace was. They really knew nothing about his life after his early boyhood. He had come home that one time when fortune so suddenly smiled upon them and they thought then that he would tell them something; but the disappointment which had followed effectually closed his lips, and he went away after a few days of fruitless search, not to approach them again till just before he took up the position of secretary to their great neighbor. Then he paid them one short and peremptory visit, during which he was able to impress upon them his importance, his reasons for changing his name, which they could not now remember, and the great necessity which this made for them not to come near him as their nephew. They had tried to do what he asked, but it had been hard. "Charity," Miss Thankful proceeded to bewail with a forgetfulness of her own share in the matter, "had not been able to keep her eyes long off the house which held, as she supposed, our double treasure." So this was all! Nothing to aid me; nothing to aid Mayor Packard. Rising in my disappointment, I prepared to leave. I had sufficient self-control and I hope good feeling not to add to their distress at this time by any unnecessary revelations of a past they were ignorant of, or the part this unhappy nephew of theirs had played and still promised to play in the lives of their immediate neighbors.

Miss Thankful squeezed my hand and Miss Charity gave me a kiss; then as she saw her sister looking aside, whispered in my ear "I want to show you something, all of Johnnie's little toys and the keepsakes he sent us when he was a good boy and loved his aunts. You will not think so badly of him then."

I let Miss Charity lead me away. A drawer held all these treasures. I looked and felt to a degree the pathos of the scene; but did not give special attention to what she thrust under my eyes till she gave me a little old letter to read, soiled and torn with the handling of many years and signed John Silverthorn Brainard. Then something in me woke and I stared at this signature, growing more and more excited as I realized that this was not the first time I had seen it, that somewhere and in circumstances which brought a nameless thrill I had looked upon it before and that—it was not one remembrance but many which came to me. What the spoken name had not recalled came at the sight of this written one. Bess! there was her long and continued watch over the house once entered by her on any and every pretext, but now shunned by her with a secret terror which could not disguise her longing and its secret attraction; her certificate of marriage; the name on this certificate—the very one I was now staring at—John Silverthorn Brainard! Had I struck an invaluable clue? Had I, through the weakness and doting fondness of this poor woman, come upon the one link which would yet lead us to identify this hollow-hearted, false and most vindictive man of great affairs with the wandering and worthless husband of the nondescript Bess, whose hand I had touched and whose errand I had done, little realizing its purport or the influence it would have upon our lives? I dared not believe myself so fortunate; it was much too like a fairy dream for me to rely on it for a moment; yet the possibility was enough to rouse me to renewed effort. After we had returned to Miss Thankful's side, I asked her, with an apology for my inexhaustible curiosity, if she still felt afraid of the thread and needle woman across the way.

The answer was a little sharp.

"It is Charity who is afraid of her," said she. She had evidently forgotten her own extravagant words to me on this subject. "Charity is timid; she thinks because this woman once hung over our brother, night and day, that she knew about this money and had persuaded herself that she has some right to it. Charity is sometimes mistaken, but she has some reason, if it is inadequate, for this notion of hers. That woman, since her dismissal after my brother's death, has never really quit this neighborhood. She worked next door in any capacity she could, whenever any of the tenants would take her; and when they would not, sewed or served in the houses near by till finally she set up a shop directly opposite its very door. But she'll never get these bonds; we shall pay her what is her due, but she'll never get any more."

"That would make her out a thief," I cried, "or—" but I thought better of uttering what was in my mind. Instead I asked how they first came to hear of her.

Miss Charity showed some flustration at this and cast her sister an appealing look; but Miss Thankful, eying her with some severity, answered me with becoming candor:

"She was a lodger in this house. We kept a few lodgers in those days—be still, Charity! Just thank God those days are over."

"A lodger?" I repeated. "Did she ever tell you where she came from?"

"Yes, she mentioned the place,—it was some town farther west. That was when we were in such trouble about our brother and how we should care for him. She could nurse him, she said, and indeed seemed very eager to do so, and we were glad to let her,—very glad, till my brother showed such fear of her and of what she might do if she once got hold of his wallet."

"You possibly did her injustice," I said. "A sick man's fancies are not always to be relied on. What did your nephew think of her? Did he share your distrust of her?"

"John? Oh, yes, I believe so. Why do we always come back to the subject of John? I want to forget him; I mean to forget him; I mean that Charity shall forget him."

"Let us begin then from this moment," I smiled; then quickly: "You knew that Bess was a married woman."

"No, we knew nothing about her."

"Not even the name she went by?"

"Oh, that was Brown."

"Brown," I muttered, turning for a second time to go. "You must think me inquisitive, but if I had not been," I added with a merry laugh, "I should never have found your bonds for you." Pressing both their hands in mine I ran hastily out of the room.

At once I crossed the street to Bess' little shop.

CHAPTER XXVIII

RESTITUTION

"Bess, why are you so white? What has happened to you in the last twenty-four hours? Have you heard from him?"

"No, no; I'm all right." But her eyes, hunted and wandering, belied her words.

I drew her hands down into mine across the table lying between us.

"I want to help you," I whispered; "I think I can. Something has happened which gives me great hope; only do me a favor first; show me, as you promised, the papers which I dug out for you."

A smile, more bitter than any tear, made her face look very hard for an instant, then she quietly led the way into the small room at the back. When we were quite alone, she faced me again and putting her hand to her breast took out the much creased, much crumpled bit of paper which was her only link to youth, to her life, and to her love.

"This is all that will interest you," said she, her eyes brimming in spite of herself. "It is my marriage certificate. The one thing that proves me an honest woman and the equal of—" she paused, biting back her words and saying instead—"of any one I see. My husband was a gentleman."

It was with trembling hands I unfolded the worn sheet. Somehow the tragedy of the lives my own had touched so nearly for the last few days had become an essential part of me.

"John Silverthorn Brainard," I read, the name identical with the one I had just seen as the early signature of the man who claimed a husband's rights over Mrs. Packard. The date with what anxiety I looked at it!—preceded by two years that of the time he united himself to Olympia Brewster. No proof of the utter falsity of his dishonorable claim could be more complete. As I folded up the paper and handed it back, Bess noted the change which had come to me. Panting with excitement she cried:

"You look happy, happy! You know something you have not told me. What? what? I'm suffocating, mad to know; speak—speak—"

"Your husband is a man not unknown to any of us. You have seen him constantly. He is—"

"Yes, yes; did he tell you himself? Has he done me so much justice? Oh, say that his heart has softened at last; that he is ready to recognize me; that I have not got to find those bonds—but you do not know about the bonds—nobody does. I shouldn't have spoken; he would be angry if he knew. Angry? and I have suffered so much from his anger! He is not a gentle man."

How differently she said this from the gentleman of a few minutes back!

"But he doesn't know that I am here," she burst out in another instant, as I hunted for some word to say. "He would kill me if he did; he once swore that he would kill me if I ever approached him or put in any claim to him till he was ready to own me for his wife and give me the place that is due me. Don't tell me that I have betrayed myself, I've been so careful; kept myself so entirely out of his eyes, even last night when I saw the doctor go in and felt that it was for him, and pictured him to myself as dying without a word from me or a look to help me bear the pain. He was ill, wasn't he?—but he got better. I saw him come out, very feeble and uncertain. Not like himself, not like the strong and too, too handsome man who has wrung my heart in his hand of steel,—wrung it and thrown it away."

Sobs shook her and she stopped from lack of power to utter either her terror or her grief. But she looked the questions she could no longer put, and compassionating her misery, I gently said:

"Your love has been fixed upon a very unstable heart; but you have rights which must yet insure you his support. There is some one who will protect these rights and protect you in your efforts to substantiate them."

"His aunt," she put in, shaking her head. "She can do nothing, unless—" Her excitement became abnormal. "Have they found the money?" she shrieked; "have they—have they found the money?"

I could not deceive her; she had seen it in my eye.

"And they will—"

"Hardly," I whispered. "He has displeased them; they can not be generous to him now."

Her hopes sank as if the very basis of her life had been taken away.

"It was my only hope," she murmured. "With that money in my hand—some, any of it, I could have dared his frown and won in a little while his good will, but now—I can only anticipate rebuff. There is nothing for me to hope for now. I must continue to be Bess, the thread and needle woman."

"I did not say that the one to reinstate you was Miss Quinlan."

"Who then? who then?"

"Mayor Packard."

And then I had to tell her.

We all know the results of the election by which Governor Packard holds his seat, but few persons outside of those mentioned in this history know why the event of his homecoming from a trip he made to Minnesota brought a brighter and more lasting light into his wife's eyes than the news of his astonishing political triumph.

He had substantiated facts by which Mr. Steele's claims upon Mrs. Packard were annulled and Bess restored to her rights, if not to her false husband's heart and affections. There are times, though, when I do not even despair of the latter; constant illness is producing a perceptible change in the man, and it seemed to me, from what Mrs. John Brainard told me one day after she had been able, through the kindness of the Misses Quinlan, to place the amount of one of the bonds in his hands, that his eyes were beginning to learn their true lesson and that he would yet find charm in his long neglected wife. It was not to be wondered at, for with hope and the advantages of dress with which the Misses Quinlan now took pleasure in supplying her, she was gradually becoming an unusually fine woman.

I remained with Mrs. Packard till they left town for the capital; remained to enjoy to the full the joy of these reunited hearts, and to receive the substantial reward which they insisted on bestowing upon me. One of the tasks with which I whiled away the many hours in which I found myself alone was the understanding and proper mastery of the cipher which had played such a part in the evolution of the life-drama enacted before my eyes.

It was very simple. With the following diagram as a key and a single hint as to its management, you will at once comprehend its apparent intricacies:

```
AB | CD | EF          \ST/
__ |__ |__            UV\ /WX
GH | IJ | KL           / \
__|__|__              /YZ\
MN| OP| QR
```

The dot designated that the letter used was the second in the indicated division.

The hint to which I allude is this. With every other word the paper is turned in the hands toward the left. This alters the shape and direction of the angle or part of square symbolizing the several letters, and creates the confusion which interfered with my solution of its mysteries the night I subjected it, with such unsatisfactory results, to the tests which had elucidated the cryptogram in The Gold Bug.

Choose from Thousands of 1stWorldLibrary Classics By

A. M. Barnard
Ada Leverson
Adolphus William Ward
Aesop
Agatha Christie
Alexander Aaronsohn
Alexander Kielland
Alexandre Dumas
Alfred Gatty
Alfred Ollivant
Alice Duer Miller
Alice Turner Curtis
Alice Dunbar
Allen Chapman
Alleyne Ireland
Ambrose Bierce
Amelia E. Barr
Amory H. Bradford
Andrew Lang
Andrew McFarland Davis
Andy Adams
Angela Brazil
Anna Alice Chapin
Anna Sewell
Annie Besant
Annie Hamilton Donnell
Annie Payson Call
Annie Roe Carr
Annonaymous
Anton Chekhov
Archibald Lee Fletcher
Arnold Bennett
Arthur C. Benson
Arthur Conan Doyle
Arthur M. Winfield
Arthur Ransome
Arthur Schnitzler
Arthur Train
Atticus
B.H. Baden-Powell
B. M. Bower
B. C. Chatterjee
Baroness Emmuska Orczy
Baroness Orczy
Basil King
Bayard Taylor
Ben Macomber
Bertha Muzzy Bower
Bjornstjerne Bjornson

Booth Tarkington
Boyd Cable
Bram Stoker
C. Collodi
C. E. Orr
C. M. Ingleby
Carolyn Wells
Catherine Parr Traill
Charles A. Eastman
Charles Amory Beach
Charles Dickens
Charles Dudley Warner
Charles Farrar Browne
Charles Ives
Charles Kingsley
Charles Klein
Charles Hanson Towne
Charles Lathrop Pack
Charles Romyn Dake
Charles Whibley
Charles Willing Beale
Charlotte M. Braeme
Charlotte M. Yonge
Charlotte Perkins Stetson
Clair W. Hayes
Clarence Day Jr.
Clarence E. Mulford
Clemence Housman
Confucius
Coningsby Dawson
Cornelis DeWitt Wilcox
Cyril Burleigh
D. H. Lawrence
Daniel Defoe
David Garnett
Dinah Craik
Don Carlos Janes
Donald Keyhoe
Dorothy Kilner
Dougan Clark
Douglas Fairbanks
E. Nesbit
E. P. Roe
E. Phillips Oppenheim
E. S. Brooks
Earl Barnes
Edgar Rice Burroughs
Edith Van Dyne
Edith Wharton

Edward Everett Hale
Edward J. O'Biren
Edward S. Ellis
Edwin L. Arnold
Eleanor Atkins
Eleanor Hallowell Abbott
Eliot Gregory
Elizabeth Gaskell
Elizabeth McCracken
Elizabeth Von Arnim
Ellem Key
Emerson Hough
Emilie F. Carlen
Emily Bronte
Emily Dickinson
Enid Bagnold
Enilor Macartney Lane
Erasmus W. Jones
Ernie Howard Pie
Ethel May Dell
Ethel Turner
Ethel Watts Mumford
Eugene Sue
Eugenie Foa
Eugene Wood
Eustace Hale Ball
Evelyn Everett-green
Everard Cotes
F. H. Cheley
F. J. Cross
F. Marion Crawford
Fannie E. Newberry
Federick Austin Ogg
Ferdinand Ossendowski
Fergus Hume
Florence A. Kilpatrick
Fremont B. Deering
Francis Bacon
Francis Darwin
Frances Hodgson Burnett
Frances Parkinson Keyes
Frank Gee Patchin
Frank Harris
Frank Jewett Mather
Frank L. Packard
Frank V. Webster
Frederic Stewart Isham
Frederick Trevor Hill
Frederick Winslow Taylor

Friedrich Kerst
Friedrich Nietzsche
Fyodor Dostoyevsky
G.A. Henty
G.K. Chesterton
Gabrielle E. Jackson
Garrett P. Serviss
Gaston Leroux
George A. Warren
George Ade
Geroge Bernard Shaw
George Cary Eggleston
George Durston
George Ebers
George Eliot
George Gissing
George MacDonald
George Meredith
George Orwell
George Sylvester Viereck
George Tucker
George W. Cable
George Wharton James
Gertrude Atherton
Gordon Casserly
Grace E. King
Grace Gallatin
Grace Greenwood
Grant Allen
Guillermo A. Sherwell
Gulielma Zollinger
Gustav Flaubert
H. A. Cody
H. B. Irving
H.C. Bailey
H. G. Wells
H. H. Munro
H. Irving Hancock
H. R. Naylor
H. Rider Haggard
H. W. C. Davis
Haldeman Julius
Hall Caine
Hamilton Wright Mabie
Hans Christian Andersen
Harold Avery
Harold McGrath
Harriet Beecher Stowe
Harry Castlemon
Harry Coghill
Harry Houidini

Hayden Carruth
Helent Hunt Jackson
Helen Nicolay
Hendrik Conscience
Hendy David Thoreau
Henri Barbusse
Henrik Ibsen
Henry Adams
Henry Ford
Henry Frost
Henry James
Henry Jones Ford
Henry Seton Merriman
Henry W Longfellow
Herbert A. Giles
Herbert Carter
Herbert N. Casson
Herman Hesse
Hildegard G. Frey
Homer
Honore De Balzac
Horace B. Day
Horace Walpole
Horatio Alger Jr.
Howard Pyle
Howard R. Garis
Hugh Lofting
Hugh Walpole
Humphry Ward
Ian Maclaren
Inez Haynes Gillmore
Irving Bacheller
Isabel Cecilia Williams
Isabel Hornibrook
Israel Abrahams
Ivan Turgenev
J.G.Austin
J. Henri Fabre
J. M. Barrie
J. M. Walsh
J. Macdonald Oxley
J. R. Miller
J. S. Fletcher
J. S. Knowles
J. Storer Clouston
J. W. Duffield
Jack London
Jacob Abbott
James Allen
James Andrews
James Baldwin

James Branch Cabell
James DeMille
James Joyce
James Lane Allen
James Lane Allen
James Oliver Curwood
James Oppenheim
James Otis
James R. Driscoll
Jane Abbott
Jane Austen
Jane L. Stewart
Janet Aldridge
Jens Peter Jacobsen
Jerome K. Jerome
Jessie Graham Flower
John Buchan
John Burroughs
John Cournos
John F. Kennedy
John Gay
John Glasworthy
John Habberton
John Joy Bell
John Kendrick Bangs
John Milton
John Philip Sousa
John Taintor Foote
Jonas Lauritz Idemil Lie
Jonathan Swift
Joseph A. Altsheler
Joseph Carey
Joseph Conrad
Joseph E. Badger Jr
Joseph Hergesheimer
Joseph Jacobs
Jules Vernes
Julian Hawthrone
Julie A Lippmann
Justin Huntly McCarthy
Kakuzo Okakura
Karle Wilson Baker
Kate Chopin
Kenneth Grahame
Kenneth McGaffey
Kate Langley Bosher
Kate Langley Bosher
Katherine Cecil Thurston
Katherine Stokes
L. A. Abbot
L. T. Meade

L. Frank Baum
Latta Griswold
Laura Dent Crane
Laura Lee Hope
Laurence Housman
Lawrence Beasley
Leo Tolstoy
Leonid Andreyev
Lewis Carroll
Lewis Sperry Chafer
Lilian Bell
Lloyd Osbourne
Louis Hughes
Louis Joseph Vance
Louis Tracy
Louisa May Alcott
Lucy Fitch Perkins
Lucy Maud Montgomery
Luther Benson
Lydia Miller Middleton
Lyndon Orr
M. Corvus
M. H. Adams
Margaret E. Sangster
Margret Howth
Margaret Vandercook
Margaret W. Hungerford
Margret Penrose
Maria Edgeworth
Maria Thompson Daviess
Mariano Azuela
Marion Polk Angellotti
Mark Overton
Mark Twain
Mary Austin
Mary Catherine Crowley
Mary Cole
Mary Hastings Bradley
Mary Roberts Rinehart
Mary Rowlandson
M. Wollstonecraft Shelley
Maud Lindsay
Max Beerbohm
Myra Kelly
Nathaniel Hawthrone
Nicolo Machiavelli
O. F. Walton
Oscar Wilde

Owen Johnson
P.G. Wodehouse
Paul and Mabel Thorne
Paul G. Tomlinson
Paul Severing
Percy Brebner
Percy Keese Fitzhugh
Peter B. Kyne
Plato
Quincy Allen
R. Derby Holmes
R. L. Stevenson
R. S. Ball
Rabindranath Tagore
Rahul Alvares
Ralph Bonehill
Ralph Henry Barbour
Ralph Victor
Ralph Waldo Emmerson
Rene Descartes
Ray Cummings
Rex Beach
Rex E. Beach
Richard Harding Davis
Richard Jefferies
Richard Le Gallienne
Robert Barr
Robert Frost
Robert Gordon Anderson
Robert L. Drake
Robert Lansing
Robert Lynd
Robert Michael Ballantyne
Robert W. Chambers
Rosa Nouchette Carey
Rudyard Kipling
Saint Augustine
Samuel B. Allison
Samuel Hopkins Adams
Sarah Bernhardt
Sarah C. Hallowell
Selma Lagerlof
Sherwood Anderson
Sigmund Freud
Standish O'Grady
Stanley Weyman
Stella Benson
Stella M. Francis

Stephen Crane
Stewart Edward White
Stijn Streuvels
Swami Abhedananda
Swami Parmananda
T. S. Ackland
T. S. Arthur
The Princess Der Ling
Thomas A. Janvier
Thomas A Kempis
Thomas Anderton
Thomas Bailey Aldrich
Thomas Bulfinch
Thomas De Quincey
Thomas Dixon
Thomas H. Huxley
Thomas Hardy
Thomas More
Thornton W. Burgess
U. S. Grant
Upton Sinclair
Valentine Williams
Various Authors
Vaughan Kester
Victor Appleton
Victor G. Durham
Victoria Cross
Virginia Woolf
Wadsworth Camp
Walter Camp
Walter Scott
Washington Irving
Wilbur Lawton
Wilkie Collins
Willa Cather
Willard F. Baker
William Dean Howells
William le Queux
W. Makepeace Thackeray
William W. Walter
William Shakespeare
Winston Churchill
Yei Theodora Ozaki
Yogi Ramacharaka
Young E. Allison
Zane Grey

www.ingramcontent.com/pod-product-compliance
Lightning Source LLC
Chambersburg PA
CBHW050035180626
46810CB00002B/732